The First Garden

ANNE HÉBERT

Translated from the French
by Sheila Fischman

Published in 1990 by
House of Anansi Press Limited
34 Lesmill Road
Toronto, Canada
M3B 2T6

Original French edition, *Le Premier Jardin*, published in
1988 by Editions du Seuil

CANADIAN CATALOGUING IN PUBLICATION DATA

Hébert, Anne, 1916-
[Premier jardin.   English]
The first garden

Translation of: Le premier jardin.
ISBN 0-88784-158-9

I. Title.   II. Title: Premier jardin.   English.

PS8515.E24P7313 1990   C843'.54   C89-090611-4
PQ3919.2.H42P7313 1990

Typesetting: Tony Gordon Ltd.

Printed in Canada on acid-free paper.

Dudek – mistrust modern world, p.m. as obsession
with experimentation. Dislocation of traditional
elements.
Hutcheon – self reflexivity. An awareness of creating
through myth. Challenge the canon. Use of parody
& irony. Questions novel as autonomous form (mod)
or as a mirror of the world (realism).

The Beckett paradigm
Absence as metaphor
Naming and identity

All the world's a stage.

William Shakespeare

P-Modernism
—self conscious narrative — Incorporation of
other arts — Ambiguity of narrative voice.
—Characters relationship with language.
Journey motife. — Questioning of borders,
worlds.

—cultural context is foregrounded. Quebec.
—geographical setting as symbolic framework,
important in. p.m.
—allusion to "return to my native land".
—universal search for identity is foregrounded in
specific idea of search for Quebec identity.
—Discovery of city = of herself. Exterior reflects
interior.
Flora: confrontation with past Rennie: reality,
Stacey: old self. Essentially self confrontation.
—Conradian allusion, 137.
—Circular ending (all 3)
—Personal & political search for identity.
—Trial by fire (Flora & Stacey). Fire & water
imagery.
—Language is foregrounded: evocative use of
names. Intertextuality. Flora: rebirth as Naming as identity.
—Edenic imagery, employment of myth of creation
(myth is also in Laurence
p.107 — turned inside out.   p. 81 Atwood, the
seen on inside
p.132 — Apocalypse imagery.
—Flora is a mirror of herself and others

TWO LETTERS FROM A DISTANT town, posted some hours apart, in different neighbourhoods, by different persons, come at the same time to her retreat in Touraine, and determine her return to her native land.

The registry office states that her name is Pierrette Paul and that she was born in a New World city, on the feast day of Saint Peter and Saint Paul, while posters scattered across the Old World declare that her features and the lineaments of her body are those of an actress known as Flora Fontanges. *Foregrounded is the question of identity*

She has pulled up the collar of her black cloth coat and carefully hidden her hair beneath a silk square tied under the chin. Offstage she is no one. An aging woman. Bare hands. A worn suitcase. She patiently waits her turn to check her bags. She's used to it. All airports resemble one another. And the points of arrival are the same as the points of departure. This woman seems to need just one thing, the role that awaits her at the end of an anonymous runway marked off by blue lights, somewhere between heaven and earth.

The name of the city of her childhood is not listed on

1

the departures board. The flight number, the boarding gate, the landing place, everything is there except . . . Perhaps, since she left it, the city has been reabsorbed where it stands, like a puddle of water in the sun?

Her face is utterly blank as she imagines, under closed eyelids, the possible disappearance of the city, and no one would suspect that she is filled with the deepest malaise. Only her pallor might betray her, should it occur to one of the crowd of travellers to take notice of her.

She seems fascinated by the wear that has whitened the edges of her black coat pockets.

She looks up.

A tiny light blinks over gate 82.

She will spend many hours crossing the Atlantic, then land somewhere in North America before the name she fears is visible on the arrivals board, spelled out, like a true country to which she has been invited to perform a part in a play.

Once she has crossed the ocean, she'll just have to wait for a connecting flight. Unless she takes the train.

Two letters were enough to make her undertake this long journey back to where she started, where she had sworn never to set foot again; a note, actually an appeal, from her daughter Maud, and a brief letter from the artistic director of the Emérillon inviting her to play Winnie in *Happy Days*.

Nothing to declare, she thinks, stepping lightly through the security check, slinging back onto her shoulder the bag holding the paint, powder, and mirror that are essential for creating each new image of herself.

Captain Georges-Henri Levasseur welcomes you on board flight 747 . . .

She presses her face against the glass. Crosses her hands on her knees. While the land disappears, leaving no horizon. There is nothing more to be seen here. A desert.

The cottony mass of clouds is broken by the passage of the airplane. Then forms again. In the distance far below, beneath the clouds, the slack fury of the invisible sea.

She curls up on the seat. Legs folded under her. Thinks about the role of Winnie. Thinks about no one but Winnie. Is filled with the notion of Winnie's crumpled little face. She concentrates. Summons up Winnie with all her strength. Brings a very old woman into being. She stares at her, observes her, spies on her. Compares herself with Winnie. Tries to mimic her. Summons from within her, until it marks her very face, everything that is fragile, vulnerable, already ruined and susceptible to death.

She tries to pull off her boots. Fills all the space allotted to her, between her seat mate and the window. Bends down as best she can. For a moment, draws the attention of her seat mate, who is abruptly wrenched from daydreams by her cramped movements as she sheds the boots. Her narrow feet in black stockings. Slender ankles.

He looks at the woman's peculiar face. Her hair is especially surprising, with grey roots and reddish tips, like the richly-colored plumage of a partridge.

She has clearly seen the man's derisive glance, his black mustache, his thick wet lips.

I am made to be seen from a distance, she thinks, doe eyes, blood-red mouth, lit by spotlights. She must send this man away. Tell him to come back. After Flora Fontanges's grey hair has grown in and all the dyed blonde and auburn tips have fallen to the scissors. She has deliberately let it grow, stopped dying it, to give herself Winnie's grey head. At the première at the Théâtre de l'Emérillon, her seat mate can sit in the first row if he wishes. Then the metamorphosis will be complete. She will show him Winnie's face in all its decrepitude. She will speak directly to him: I am Winnie. No one will have the right to contradict her. Her seat mate will be captivated. The audience greedy and silent, as before a bullfight. Her craft is about to go on public display, and those who have seen her childlike and beautiful will watch her decay inch by inch, under the dazzling spotlights, throughout an entire summer.

She wants to sleep. Brushes her face with her hand to wipe away the traces of a role that is invading her. Will the same gesture erase the bitter fold at the corner of her mouth, those thin furrows around the eyes, and restore her firm-cheeked youth?

The presence of the sleeping man at her side makes her uneasy. His breathing close to her. Hers close to him. Their breathing mingled as if they were lying together in the same bed. An old couple bound by the seat-belt, flank against flank, forever strangers one to the other.

For the first time since her departure she wonders about the laconic note from her daughter, whom she has not seen for a year.

"I'd love to see you. Come. Kisses. Maud"

THERE IS NO TRAIN STATION NOW. A shed in the middle of a field stands in its place. The train stops in a vacant lot. Someone says this is it. They've arrived. Everyone gets out. Night. Open country. Garlands of light trace distant streets. On all sides, night. Taxis in line, motionless. Mayflies dance in headlights' beams.

There are flowers in her arms. Flowers from the artistic director of the Emérillon. He has a broad smile over pointed teeth, and small round metal-rimmed glasses. She looks for her daughter, Maud. Complains that she can't see her daughter. The director says Maud is probably waiting at the hotel. They climb into a taxi.

The director explains that the new city, half-village, half-suburb, girds the old one like a green sash. She does not hear what the man beside her is saying. At every flash of neon that indicates a motel or barbecued chicken, she shuts her eyes. Wishes she could melt into the night. *Anywhere out of this world.* Is anxious because she feels there is no life here, where she is at the moment. At the same time, it suits her. She only hopes there will be no reaction (no clash, no emotion) between the city and herself before she arrives at the hotel on rue Sainte-Anne. She does not want to remember that her false grandmother used to

5

live in the old city, that she had to go through the walls on her way to her house for lunch every Sunday.

The artistic director of the Emérillon is glad to see that the work on Flora Fontanges's beautiful face is already under way. They'll only have to exaggerate the effect with makeup and boldly accentuate her age. Then the burial in sand of a living creature can be accomplished, one grain at a time, one night at a time, at the Emérillon summer theatre, as its artistic director has dreamed of doing now for years.

margin note: life is a play

FOR A LONG TIME SHE SLEPT VERY late, in strange rooms, foreign cities. For many years she experienced the trepidation of a woman awakening in the dark, unsure where she is. Utter panic at not knowing, for a moment, who she is. Now she's used to it though. Everything works out in the end. She just has to retrace the order of objects in the room before she even opens her eyes. Determine some precise reference points. Yesterday's clothes tossed onto a chair, the location of the window in relation to the bed. Grope patiently until she finds the concealed switch for the bedside lamp. Confront the unknown city head on, in the steady light of day.

The little square under her window is spattered with sunlight. Freshly washed calèches, their red wheels glistening with water, horses with their noses in bags of oats. Calèche drivers hail one another. The aroma of french-fried potatoes joins the strong smell of horse manure.

This is the present at its liveliest. All the church bells in the city compete as they sound the angelus, great gusts of sound. The cannon at the Citadel thunders noon. The inhabitants of the upper town set their watches and clocks by that cannon.

Flora Fontanges remembers nothing. She must struggle to remind herself that her daughter was not at the station or the hotel last night.

HE IS FACING HER, LEANING TO-
wards her across a small table on the terrace of a café.
She leans over too because of the noise from the street,
while her tea gets cold and he finishes his milk. He tells
her again that Maud's been gone for two weeks now and
he's freaking out, especially at night. There is a drop of
milk at the corner of his mouth. His voice is low and
drawling, as if muffled.

Flora Fontanges looks at the boy who sleeps with her
daughter and doesn't believe he could be in the grip of
any amorous difficulty. He orders another glass of milk.
He stretches in the sun. As she watches, he is consoled
by the pleasure this day gives him. His long legs under
the table extend to the one next to them. He is trying
hard to think about Maud. Makes a face like a child on
the verge of tears.

Horses clomping along the Grande-Allée, calèches
crammed with tourists, long American cars passing the
calèches, stains of sunlight among the leaves, sunlight
shimmering on leaves. She hears herself say:

"Have you two quarrelled?"

He frowns but it is erased from his brow at once as if
nothing, no line or fold, could last on his smooth face.

9

"Quarrelled? Maud and I? Never!"

Then says he doesn't know why Maud went away.

He seems to be searching for a reason for Maud's departure but it escapes him, like a mosquito in the dark that you can hear but cannot catch. His fine, innocent face, vaguely perplexed.

His name is Raphaël. He is twenty years old. During the summer, he tells American tourists about the city. Last year he was studying history at the university. For almost a year now he has been living with Maud, who has been a runaway since childhood.

Flora Fontanges thinks, nothing ever changes. If Maud has disappeared she is bound to come back as she did the other times. But though she tries to reassure herself, something in the air that she is struggling to breathe is filled with menace.

This boy across from her seems to be fighting to reject the *joie de vivre* that comes naturally to him. Again, a vague frown. His slow, flat voice slurs a little, as if he were talking to himself.

"Sometimes Maud, her face, when she thought nobody was looking at her, when she wasn't looking at us either, it was as if she was offended by something, some remote offence she wasn't even aware of, but it would show on her face just like that, in passing, for no reason, like a shadow . . ."

She felt herself under accusation by Raphaël, she, the mother, the source of her daughter's affections, of everything that began in the heart of that child. A little more and this boy would tell her about the first offence committed against Maud in the mists of time, when Maud had neither speech nor clear features.

"What was Maud like when she was little?"

Why not evoke the little girl smelling of talcum powder who would draw herself up on tiptoe to kiss her mother as she comes off stage? The dressing room is full of flowers with letters from admirers tucked among them. Flora Fontanges is wearing a red velvet gown, her bare shoulders moist with sweat, and sparkling beads are woven into her black chignon. The little girl wears a smocked dress of Liberty print. Her hair is black like her mother's. She is three, or perhaps five years old.

This idyllic apparition disturbs Flora Fontanges. She would rather cling to a more recent image of her daughter, of the obstinate adolescent who has just run away for the first time. She speaks to Raphaël as if she were addressing, through him, someone hidden far away in the city. She finds her clear actress's voice, accustomed to song and speech broken by dramatic pauses.

"There's nothing to understand. My daughter's face is as impenetrable as stone. It's impossible to know if she's hungry or thirsty, hot or cold, sick or well, if she wants fruit or chocolate, a leather jacket or ice skates. Her desires seem inaccessible even to her."

He listens. He is surprised at the voice, warm and vehement, as if a ventriloquist were expressing herself through this ageless unassuming woman. He says he'll go to see her act in *Happy Days*.

She looks at the Victorian houses, now transformed into cafés and restaurants. She wonders when it began, all these parasols, brightly coloured awnings, small tables, these chairs planted as if on a beach all down the length of the Grande-Allée.

Raphaël is engrossed in his glass of milk. His long lashes cast shadows on his cheeks. He raises his head. Eyes the color of agates. If Maud and Raphaël have something in common it cannot be merely childhood.

She says:

"Maud was hardly more than a child when she left me. What's she like now?"

"Tall and pale, with black hair, straight and very long, long enough to sit on. Magnificent!"

For a moment Flora Fontanges seems to be gazing at a stranger who stands before her, his height and beauty theatrical, formidable.

"A year ago, Maud went away and I had no word from her for two months."

He rests both hands on the table, brings his face quite close to hers. He blinks in the sun. His voice suddenly abrupt:

"Did you or didn't you go crazy during those two months?"

Flora Fontanges pulls back. Half-hidden by her dark glasses. Strives inwardly to keep at a distance anyone who can touch her and wound her.

They decide not to notify the police, to wait. They are standing in the summer light. She has already paid the bill. He says he didn't realize she was so tall.

He watches her as she disappears along the Grande-Allée.

F<small>LORA</small> F<small>ONTANGES</small> <small>WALKS</small> <small>DOWN</small> streets that seem foreign to her and is reassured that they feel foreign. As long as she keeps her distance, nothing untoward can happen to her. As far as her daughter Maud is concerned, even if she were to meet her at a street corner she's not sure that she'd recognize her.

The Grande-Allée with its tawdry theatrical finery extends as far as the St. Louis Gate. Tourists and passing civil servants stroll the sidewalks. Three quick stops and they're gone. Were not born here. Will not die here. Just passing, all of them. To sleep here for a night or two. Eat and drink. Smoke a joint. Cruise girls or boys. Take a calèche ride. No births or deaths (except for accidents) inside the stone houses daubed with color. But where are the people? The real ones? Those whose lives are tied to the dark woodwork, the nasty cellars, the exhausting staircases, the stacked-up storeys, the roaring fireplaces. Have they gone away, are they sleeping their final sleep walled up inside these stone mansions with their broad bow-windows?

More than anything else, Flora Fontanges is afraid of awakening phantoms, of having to play a role among ghosts.

everything in her
life is false

13

She quickens her pace, strides faster and faster. As if she too could join the race. Carefully avoids the St. Louis Gate. Will not see today the grey house fronts on the Esplanade or the tall mansion of her false grandmother, which they have transformed into a hotel. As she walks past the old tennis courts of the parliament buildings, the sight of the distant mountains and sky briefly, surprisingly, touches her heart.

Rᴀᴘʜᴀëʟ ᴄʟɪᴍʙᴇᴅ ᴅɪʀᴇᴄᴛʟʏ ᴜᴘ to Flora Fontanges's room. He knocked on the door and called out: "It's me, Raphaël." She is wearing a dressing gown and her hair is wet. Has been lying low. Is furious at being disturbed. Raphaël calls out again, louder: "It's me, Raphaël." She opens the door a crack and sees that he's not alone. He tells her Céleste is a friend of Maud's, that she's just arrived from the North Shore.

Céleste carries her house on her back. Like a big ant, bent under the weight of her pack. A folded tent, a sleeping bag, an alcohol burner, tins, smoked meat, salted crackers, a first-aid kit, mosquito repellent, Mexican boots, and some books on ethnology. She drops her burden on the floor and rubs her shoulders. Laughs, showing all her long, strong teeth. She is very tall, thin, and bony, wearing too-short shorts and enormous sneakers. Straight blonde bangs fall over her eyes. Her legs, her arms, her neck are covered with mosquito bites. She says that the North Shore is fantastic, but the mosquitoes are a real drag.

Céleste ensconces herself in the easy chair, her legs apart, eyes half-shut. She declares that civilization has its good points and that bourgeois chairs are very comfortable. She laughs. She talks about Maud. Says "us girls," and seems to want to exclude the rest of humankind.

"Even if I knew where Maud is I wouldn't tell you or Raphaël. There's real loyalty between us girls. Mothers are as macho as guys, everybody knows that."

An image of Maud suddenly comes to her, here in the stale air of the small hotel room at the end of the afternoon. She could simply reach out her arm in this heat and touch the sleeping form of her daughter, here on her child's bed. Her eyes would be shut, she'd be peaceful and calm, wrapped in her mystery, guarded in sleep, and safe from the entire world.

Flora Fontanges lingers over that image, the most reassuring of all, wishing it would last forever, of the childhood, gone for good, of her daughter Maud. She vaguely hears the voices of Raphaël and Céleste flying over her head like stray bullets.

"The last time I saw Maud was before I left for the North Shore. She seemed really uptight, you know how she gets?"

Raphaël shakes his head obstinately.

Céleste laughs, her head tipped against the chair back.

"Poor Raphaël, you've never really looked at her. I've never seen such a girl as uptight as Maud."

Raphaël stares at the wall as if he were searching for his words there among the flowers on the wallpaper.

"We were supposed to be leaving for Charlevoix in three days. Everything was ready. I don't get it."

Céleste shrugs and says no one understands anything about anything but that she, Céleste Larivière, has her own personal little light to shed on the matter of Amerindian women, which will be the subject of her thesis.

Céleste asks if she can take a bath. Shuts herself inside the bathroom. Then sweeps back into the room. Parades around naked. Blonde head, black armpits and pubis, arms and legs inordinately long. Roots around in her possessions. Kneels on the floor. Goes back in the bathroom. Sprays herself all over with Flora Fontanges's perfume. Shouts through the door that she reeks of old actress.

Now she is in the bedroom again, draped in a bath towel. She gurgles with pleasure. Goes back to the chair. Shuts her eyes. Abandons herself entirely to the well-being that follows a bath. Meditates. Prolongs the ecstasy. Puts off as long as possible the moment when she must act and move.

Wearing white shorts and a very green T-shirt she says "bye" and is on her way, her burden on her back. Raphaël wishes her good luck, then turns back to Flora Fontanges. Explains that Céleste has just enough time to find shelter for the night. He says it's quite possible that she'll sleep at Eric's place. Flora Fontanges asks who Eric is. Raphaël says it's a long story.

She wipes up the bathroom. Calls and asks for clean towels.

SHE HAS HAD HER HAIR CUT VERY
short. The multicoloured ends strew the hairdresser's floor.
Now here she is with a grey head like a little bird's.

She is facing the artistic director of the Emérillon, who
cannot grasp what it is about Flora Fontanges that has
changed so profoundly. His name is Gilles Perrault. He
has washed-out blue eyes whose colour fades into his
withered cheeks. He takes off his little round glasses and
tries to see Flora Fontanges through a myopic haze. She
has changed her appearance without consulting him—the
director of the play and artistic director of the theatre.
He is upset and disconcerted, as if the docile actress from
Happy Days had suddenly escaped him, allowing herself
to work on another role in secret. He replaces his glasses
and notes that Flora Fontanges's smile is too charming
for Winnie. He must forbid her to smile once rehearsals
get under way.

Flora Fontanges tells herself that now that she's made
herself look like Joan of Arc at the stake, she could very
well act out the passion of a nineteen-year-old virgin
stripped bare at the fire that will reduce her to ashes.
Raphaël and Céleste would be invited to the performance,
in perfect collusion with her raging youth and tragic

18

destiny. She would make them live the *Real Trial of Joan* quite straightforwardly, sparing them nothing. To do so she need only dip into the well-springs of her own life, where a great savage fire still burns and makes her scream in her sleep. Of all her roles, that of Joan was the one that was most applauded during the course of her career. But could she play it again, in this city, and not risk losing her life in it?

She has left Gilles Perrault and is heading now for the Boule d'Or on rue Saint-Jean, where she is to meet Raphaël.

- the idea of loosing oneself in fire.

THEY ARE ALL THERE WITH
Raphaël on the café terrace, Maud's friends, the ones
from the commune. They've pulled two tables together.
They are drinking milk or orange juice. They've seen her
coming from a distance, with her shoulder bag and her
haircut, like Joan of Arc at the stake. Raphaël makes the
introductions. He looks at Flora Fontanges's hairdo. He
says:

"You look younger."

This glorious summer. Only, don't breathe too deeply,
and be careful to expel the air after it has revived the
blood. Just live in the moment. Confine herself to the
present only. As if she were one of Maud's friends at the
table on the narrow terrace of a café on rue Saint-Jean.
She has already looked as far as she can, the full length
of the street, as far as the Eglise du Faubourg. As if to
make sure that nothing threatening could come from that
direction.

They are all talking at once. Trying to explain about
rue Saint-Jean on summer Saturday nights. Groups of
young people piled onto the terraces. Passersby all on the
same side of the street, no one's ever figured out why.
Cars pass at ten miles an hour. There's plenty of time to

20

shop, to select without getting out of the car the girl or
boy you want.

They laugh. They are giving Flora Fontanges a warm
welcome because she's an actress and she's come from
Europe. They decide to show her around the city. They
treat her like a model tourist. The usual sites. Montcalm's
house, the treasure-houses of the Ursulines and of the
Hôtel-Dieu. At the Maison de la Fort someone in the
shadows, among the mock-ups all in a row, gives an account
of the 1759 battle, scarcely a few minutes long, in the
course of which the city and the entire country were lost.

interest in national identity.

At that very moment the inevitable occurs. Here is the
Esplanade, and the grey façade, the window-frames now
painted blue, of 45 rue d'Auteuil. Surely no past life can
still persist inside. Tap the stone with a finger. There is
only emptiness. The echo of emptiness. Hollow stone. The
past now a mere pebble. There's no risk that a tall old
woman in black will appear at the window and lift a curtain
of guipure lace to spy on Flora Fontanges and point at
her. No harsh old woman's voice can seep out the window
and pronounce a death sentence on a little girl who was
rescued from the Hospice Saint-Louis.

"You'll never make a lady of her."

Flora Fontanges tells herself that no one is more deaf
than she who does not want to hear. She asks for a
cigarette. No one around her has one. Someone mentions
pollution.

They are sitting in the grass of the little park on the
Esplanade. She is on a bench facing them. They raise
their heads towards her, expecting who knows what magical
discourse. Isn't she an actress, doesn't she possess the
power to change ordinary words into resounding, quickening speech?

She wishes she could meet their expectations. That she
could recite a beautiful poem for them very softly, her

voice velvet against their ears, requiring keen attention, a lover's fervour. Hold them spellbound, there at the peak of existence. To be, for a moment, that point of light balancing on the horizon that sways and falls in a spray of foam.

She drops her head. Concentrates. In the utter poverty of the moment. Gathers up her poverty like a gift. Now she is merely a tall shorn woman in the summer sun. Given over to all these gazes that surround her. To this wild expectation. In the merciful night. Joan in her is submitting to her trial and her death. She has just recanted. She trembles. Her voice is now a taut thread, breaking.

"I was so afraid of being burned . . ."

Suddenly Flora Fontanges is no longer master of the sounds, the smells, the images that jostle within her. The acrid smoke, a small girl coughing and choking in the shadows, the crackling of hell close by, the suffocating heat, dread in its original purity. She hears herself say for the second time, very softly but so distinctly that every word can be read on her lips:

"I was so afraid of being burned . . ."

The brief sentence catches them by surprise, the silence holds them absolutely still for a moment, heads raised towards her, then they shake themselves and look at one another, amazed, afraid she's mocking them. Such a brief remark, taken out of context, having its own effect and producing such an effect on them, must be a sign of some misunderstanding, or a spell.

She runs her hand over her brow to erase Joan and her trial by fire. Discovers her own face, worn and dull. Says that she wants to go home. Raphaël at her feet hasn't budged. He wishes this would go on forever—the expression on the face of Flora Fontanges, the sound of her voice. The drama, her terror. A kind of nervous voracity. He pleads with her:

"Don't go right away."

She is standing in the little park on the Esplanade, surrounded by boys and girls, wearing no makeup, all prestige stripped off like a mask, a tired and aging woman.

Céleste says she hasn't the faintest idea where she'll sleep tonight. No one knows who mentions there are twin beds in Flora Fontanges's room in the hotel on rue Sainte-Anne.

—her life is mixed up in the roles she plays.

CÉLESTE FELL ASLEEP ALMOST AT once after declaring that a real bed, even if you aren't making love in it, is fantastic.

Flora Fontanges is awake in the dark. The strange breathing at her side takes up too much space in the bedroom, sucks all the surrounding air. Flora Fontanges feels as if she's suffocating. She wonders where her own daughter is sleeping tonight.

In the morning she had to ask Céleste to leave. The girl jumped out of the bed as if there were a spring in the hollow of her back.

"Oh, these clean sheets are so soft, they're fabulous, but I'm scared I'd be selling my soul. I'll go now."

She left half her belongings in the room.

SHE PRESSES HER THIN HANDS together. Leafs through the script of *Happy Days* as if Winnie's fate no longer concerned her. Wishes she were indestructible and hard as a stone. This role, though, is unexpected. She has been brought out of retirement for this, of all roles, like a plant moved from shade into the light of day, after being required for so long to be extravagantly made up, glaringly lit, so that none of the expression of her face or body would be lost, from any seat in the theatre. And then little by little she had to put away greasepaint and powder, tears and the burst of joy and bracing hysteria. Stripped of her reason for being, she began growing roses and dahlias in Touraine, where she was in the process of converting an old dovecote, when her daughter disappeared again, like a bird on the horizon taking flight.

She decides to stop thinking about Winnie, to keep Winnie off to the side for a little while yet, like her own old age that is now approaching.

The first reading with her partner, under the washed-out gaze of the artistic director of the Emérillon, has been set for July the third.

RAPHAËL INSISTS ON SHOWING HER the city as if she had never before set foot there. Perhaps now she will escape from what she knows about the city and be satisfied with Raphaël's version? *Anywhere out of this world,* she tells herself. She is here to play a role in the theatre. She will play it. Then go away and live the rest of her life somewhere else. Unless her daughter suddenly appears. Her arms around her neck. Her cool cheek against her own.

Raphaël, like a proper accredited guide, has brought a map of the city. Flora Fontanges bends over the unfolded map spread out flat on the bed. She is looking for the Côte de la Couronne and for Saint-Roch. She crosses out the whole district with a stroke of her pen. She sets conditions. There are forbidden places where she will never go. Let Raphaël be warned.

As far as rue Plessis is concerned, there's nothing to worry about. She has seen distinctly on the map that the street no longer exists, nor do the streets nearby. The whole neighbourhood has been torn down, the maze of little streets and lanes, the proper houses and the hovels behind the splendid mansions on the Grande-Allée. But what has become of the people who once lived there? Did they make a bonfire of their old despair, a jumble of old cooking pots, sagging mattresses, grimy rags? Who blew down, like a house of cards, Mr. Smith's candy store? What little girl lingers in the mind of Flora Fontanges, clearly uttering a phrase that has no relation to the worn-out adult Flora Fontanges has become?

"Please, Sir, a penny's worth of licorice."

A little package of short black sticks, hollow like macaroni, tied with red string, a minuscule bundle of sweets, is displayed in Mr. Smith's window. Desire recaptured. Lust intact. Again she hears the little girl's voice in her head:

"Please, Sir, a penny's worth of licorice?"

He begs her to come with him. Says it's a beautiful day, that it's almost noon.

What holds her back, keeps her motionless in the middle of the room, has nothing to do with Raphaël or with the weather. It has to do with an image from the past.

She sees quite clearly a cut-glass doorknob that glitters strangely on rue Plessis with its dark façades. Flora Fontanges will never be able to describe the peculiar beauty of this object, the prism of colors thrown off by each facet, all turning to violet with the passing of time. Only turn that gleaming knob, very carefully, and you will gain access to the whole apartment of M. and Mme Eventurel, who have adopted a little girl who was rescued from the Hospice Saint-Louis.

"Are you coming, Madame Fontanges?"

Raphaël is growing impatient. He is young and handsome, here at midday, in the city he thinks he knows like no one else in the world. She is no longer altogether with him. She has been busy within herself, in search of images that disturb her.

This must be what it is like to lapse into second childhood: a little barrier in the brain gives way and the past surges in, dense as mercury, overtaking the present and drowning it, while death prevails over life, as it says in the law.

T HE MIDDAY GLARE ON ALL THINGS.
The upper town held up by its cape, covered with green tufts
like the countryside, there at the crest of the walls where the
Citadel is perched against the sky. Below, the Plains of
Abraham. And beneath it the river, oceanic here, and
smelling of mud, oil, and tar, bathes moss-covered wharves.
All the bells are pealing.

Raphaël can only list the names of churches along their
way, as if they were dead old women obliterated by the
sun's dazzle. While Flora Fontanges wonders if there is
still someone in each church who answers to the name
of God. There was a time when God made rash promises
behind the grey stone façades. That was a time of certainty.
Once the portal was open you knew what to expect. An
illuminated red lamp signalled the real presence. A blinking
flame, the Pentecostal sign, hanging near the altar, and
one knew at once that the burning bush existed, shut
away inside the sanctuary. God dwelt there, concealing
Himself out of pity for us, because of the unbearable
radiance of His face.

"Raphaël, do you believe in God?"

Raphaël says he doesn't know, he's never thought about it.

"What about you?"

She says she doesn't know either.

28

SHE STAYED WITH HIM TILL EVENING, exhausted, scarcely listening to him, given over to her own memory, like a child who can no longer follow her own thoughts.

Raphaël says that their greatest dream, his and Maud's, was to live one entire day without wasting a moment of it. Paying utmost attention to the passage of time over the city, as if they had found themselves transformed into a sundial that could pick up the slightest vibration of light, from morning till night, their vigilance and their joy in the passing moment never flagging.

He laughs. He says it's a dream, that he and Maud have tried several times, but never made it because they couldn't concentrate.

"One day, maybe, I'll know how to live life to the full, I'll be strong enough not to waste it. Perhaps with you, Madame Fontanges. It's already started with us, since noon today. But you're too distracted."

She says she's tired and would like to go home.

He appears disconcerted, sheepish, like a child who's been punished. He insists that she stay with him.

"Don't leave yet, it's not even dark. You must watch the night now, from Dufferin Terrace. You'll see. The day's not done until it topples into the dark. Emptying its pockets before going to bed. We create a void. In our heads. In our bodies. We throw everything overboard. We see the darkness coming in all around us, creeping over us little by little. Before we sink for good and fall asleep till morning, like a sort of death. You must watch the night arrive, watch it spread out all around. You must see it, Madame Fontanges, you must . . ."

A huge sky, extremely high, not yet completely black, glows with a thousand points of light. The river, which has not yet shed its own light, reflects the sky and casts up glitter from all its gleaming waves. A confused stamping of hooves on planks, the warmth and sound of passing lives. Dufferin Terrace pours out its nocturnal crowd under the summer sky. People from the upper town join those from the lower town on the wooden promenade. Two currents meet, collide and mingle on the resonant boards, like the movement of the river when sweet water meets salt, briefly blurring, then each follows its briny course.

They have waited until the sky turns perfectly black. Raphaël on her arm, like a son who might have brought her out for a stroll. He's tall enough to be seen from a distance. Close up, you can see his handsome face. Girls eye him as they pass. Their bright blouses, their mischievous eyes, their mouths, desirable and desiring.

"Hey, good-looking, where are you spending the night?"

Raphaël seems to want to melt into the crowd that is brushing against him. He says it's like salt water, it holds him up. Amid the movement of the crowd he is like a fish in water. She exists without desire in a world that is only desire. Throbbing life rushes in around her on all sides.

IT IS A SUMMER DAY WITHOUT RADIANCE, the sun half-hidden behind layers of cloud, turning them white-hot. The sky weighs on our heads like a burning, chalky lid.

The lower town is baking, its freshly cleaned stones, its half-dressed tourists. The Théâtre de l'Emérillon stands behind the Place Royale. A shady opening, cool and dark. Like breathing the air of a cellar or a sacristy.

Flora Fontanges has been summoned by the director, for a bit of a tryout he says, half closing his myopic eyes. This bit of a tryout consists of placing Flora Fontanges on the stage, with no props or partner, no spotlight or curtain, after ascertaining that the theatre is totally deserted. A private meeting for the director and Flora Fontanges. To isolate Flora Fontanges in the void. Examine her from every angle like a living germ under a microscope. To capture her at the moment of her metamorphosis, this role must seep into her little by little. With no script or voice, no motion or makeup, in the utmost nudity, so that Winnie may emerge into the light and become visible on the face of Flora Fontanges and in her body, which will shrink and shrivel before our very eyes.

She calls upon a lifetime of experience, laden with age

31

and lost illusions. She has access to things she does not yet know, that are only hinted at among the shadows of passing time. Flora Fontanges is already consumed by eternity, given over altogether to the role that inhabits her and possesses her.

Slight particles of dust are visible, stirring in the beam of light that comes through the open door.

The director has arranged for her to stand in the very centre of the beam, under a delicate sifting of dust. He adjusts his little gold-rimmed spectacles. He looks, as if through a magnifying lens, at the woman alone on the stage, in the wan light and the swirling dust. Seated now on a canvas folding stool, she bows her head and stares at the veins of her hands, spread flat on her knees. As Flora Fontanges concentrates, the veins swell and stand out more and more clearly and blue against her pale hands.

Soon there will be just a little old lady, wizened and mute, her presence revealed only by its dryness, like a heap of brittle bones.

Gilles Perrault pays close attention, as if life and death were being played out to his orders, here before him. He commands her in an exhausted voice, barely audible:

"Show your arms now. I want to see your bare arms raised and crossed above your head. Remember, you are old, very old . . ."

She sheds her linen jacket and raises her bare arms above her head. These are indeed Winnie's arms as the director has dreamed of them. He swallows, sighs with satisfaction.

The time hangs heavy. A few seconds? Minutes? An old woman keeps her old arms raised endlessly above her head. The director standing motionless at her feet, in the front row of the theatre, takes great pleasure in the sight.

A few onlookers have gathered in the open door, blocking off the light from outside, surprised at how cool it is in the theatre. Gilles Perrault claps his hands. Flora Fontanges brings down her arms. Slowly comes back to herself. Lazarus emerging from the tomb may have experienced this, the extreme slowness of the entire being who must learn again how to live.

She dons her jacket again as if doing so were the hardest thing in the world.

Her daughter's face chooses this very moment to appear, when Flora Fontanges, defenceless, seems to be struggling to extricate herself from a pile of dead wood. Here it is now, raised up to her, childish and pink, the little lost face. Moist black eyes, the whites nearly blue. She shrinks back. A line that is not in the play lingers in her.

"What an idea, to bring my daughter here at such a time. I'm drained, dead . . ."

She says again, aloud:

"I am drained, dead . . ."

The features of Maud as a child fade away to make room for the director's stooped figure.

"Amazing! You're absolutely amazing!"

He has taken off his glasses. His blue eyes are misted with tears. He cannot see two steps ahead of him. While she begins to smile, without his seeing. The transfiguring smile pushes away the role of Winnie, makes her resemble a beaming actress bowing slightly, after escaping once again the danger of death.

"It's so wonderful to act!"

And she knows no other words, seeks no other words to express her plenitude and her bliss.

SHE TOOK HER LEAVE OF THE director of the Emérillon after he reminded her of the date, July third, for the first reading of *Happy Days*. She is free until the third of July.

Now she is wandering through the streets with their old restored houses. She sets Winnie aside. Cleanses herself of Winnie's unattractive face and ravaged body, which cling to her skin. She is once more no one in particular. She is neither young nor old. No longer fully alive. Except for an insistent desire for a cool shower and an icy drink.

She is alone by the side of the river in the lower part of the city, where everything began three centuries ago. It resembles a theatre set. She is looking for a street name which is also the name of a woman, one that Raphaël told her about.

Barbe Abbadie, she repeats to herself, as if she were calling someone in the dark. She is seeking a woman's name to inhabit. To shine forth anew in the light.

She seeks and does not find. Raphaël must have been mistaken.

"I am drained, dead . . ."

Her daughter Maud shows herself again. A centre part and heavy black hair on either side of round cheeks.

Maud's voice says that numbers are alive. She is a mathematics student and a runaway.

Flora Fontanges wishes she could chase away the image of her daughter. Asks for mercy. Settles into her fatigue. Begs for time to recover from Winnie's despair. Is already in search of another role.

The damp heavy heat makes her clothes stick to her skin. Her mouth is dry as if she has a fever.

None of the streets near Place Royale bears the name of Barbe Abbadie. Raphaël has probably been dreaming.

Starting with a name that has scarcely emerged from Raphaël's dream then, why cannot Flora Fontanges in turn discover a living creature named Barbe Abbadie, decked out in just her name, as in a brilliant skin, at the beginning of the world?

So many times already, throughout her career, she has let herself be seduced by the titles of plays that are women's names before she knew anything about the script. Names to dream on, to ripen a role in secret, before the lines burst out, sharp and precise.

Hedda Gabler, Adrienne Lecouvreur, Mary Tudor, Yerma, Phaedra, Miss Julie.

A name, just a name, that already exists powerfully within her.

Barbe Abbadie, she repeats to herself, when the sky abruptly turns black.

You can trace the first drops of rain as they fall slowly, one by one, widely spaced like dark stains on the fieldstones and the rubble-stones of the old houses that line the Place Royale.

All the patina of life on the walls and on the roofs has been carefully scraped off and wiped away. These are dwellings from another time, as fresh as brand-new toys.

The river is there, sputtering with rain against the wharfs.

Soon, torrents of dark water lash the city.

A café crowded with people dripping rain, their hair

plastered down, faces like the drowned.

Raphaël has joined Flora Fontanges. They talk about Barbe Abbadie. Wonder what good deeds Barbe Abbadie might have done, to have been given a street, and what evil she might have done to have the street taken from her almost immediately. Together they decide on Barbe Abbadie's age, her marital status, her life and her death.

Thirty years old, a merchant husband who owns two ships and a large shop on the rue Sault-au-Matelot, four children with a fifth due shortly, an account book impeccably maintained, a shop filled with the good smells of woollen cloth, of silk, muslin, and canvas. There is talk of ells, of *sols* and gold *louis,* in the cool half-light of the shop. Barbe Abbadie reigns over the shop and the house. With every step her magnificent legs set aswirl a full rigging of petticoats and skirts. Her deep frills are recognizable from afar. Gripped by fear and respect, servants and shopgirls listen to her move from bedroom to corridor, from corridor to staircase, all the day long.

As she sips her iced tea, Flora Fontanges imagines the hands and eyes of Barbe Abbadie. Dark blue eyes, soft strong hands. She tries to capture Barbe Abbadie, full face and in profile. Small nose, round chin. She tries to imagine the sound of her voice, swallowed up long ago by the air of time. Flora Fontanges pays no attention now to Raphaël sitting opposite her. She dreams of taking over Barbe Abbadie's desiccated heart, of hanging it between her own ribs, of bringing it back to life again, an extra heart, the vermilion blood pumped into it from her own chest.

Raphaël enters into the game. He says they must pin down the time when Barbe Abbadie lived. Why not the mid-seventeenth century, say 1640 for example?

Flora Fontanges thinks of the odour of Barbe Abbadie, which must have been powerful, at a time when people didn't wash much. Under Barbe Abbadie's arms and skirts, her cloth-merchant husband must have choked in savage ecstasy.

They must dress her, this woman, offer her fine linen and lace, gowns and fichus, headdresses and bonnets, and a set of keys complete with the one to the salt and the wine, the one for the sheets and towels, and the tiny golden key to the jewel casket.

Raphaël talks about the museum just next to them, that has many objects and utensils used by the country's first settlers. As soon as the rain has stopped they must go and look for Barbe Abbadie's vanished household: a pestle for salt in its mortar, a wheel for spinning wool, perhaps even the set of keys that provided access to her whole life.

It's a matter of getting your hands on the right key, and Flora Fontanges appropriates for herself straightaway the soul and the body of Barbe Abbadie. She takes from it words and gestures, she causes Barbe Abbadie to hear, see, listen, laugh and cry, eat and drink, make love every night, tumbling happily with her husband in unbleached linen sheets.

Flora Fontanges grows sad. She catches a glimpse of the end of Barbe Abbadie, dead in childbirth in 1640, in the big bed made for feasts of love, in the master bedroom on the first floor of a fine stone house at 6, rue Sault-au-Matelot. Now that house is filled with the screams of a woman in labour and the cries of a child, and with the rumble of raucous sobbing by a man who believes he has lost everything.

Flora Fontanges beams with the life and death of Barbe Abbadie. She is powerful now, inescapable, at the height of her confidence. Glows with all her fire. She leans across the table to Raphaël.

She is and is not Flora Fontanges.

"Raphaël dear, how you're staring at me, how you listen! I am Barbe Abbadie and I'm looking at you too, and listening to you. How old are you, Raphaël dear?"

He says he's just twenty.

Flora Fontanges laughs.

He murmurs:

"You're marvellous."

His whole body moves abruptly. He brings his face down close to Flora Fontanges's hand. Tries to kiss it. A slight movement of the wrist, barely perceptible, and her hand turns over, palm up, soft and warm under Raphaël's caress.

She says that's called "faire larirette" and that it's always the first step in love between Barbe Abbadie and her husband. A tiny little kiss on the palm of the hand.

She laughs.

"Don't worry, Raphaël dear, it's only theatre."

A few drops of rain lengthen and trail on the windowpane. Conversations in the café rise a notch, as if everyone, freed now of watching the rain fall, were suddenly starting to talk at once.

Flora Fontanges gradually calms down, withdraws into herself. Plays with the strap of her bag. Says she wants to go home. Raphaël wonders if he has dreamed. An ordinary woman is standing and waiting for him to finish his orange juice.

He sips it slowly. Forgets Barbe Abbadie. Accepts only the present. He is content and pleased with it. The acid, sugary taste of orange. He sees on the table before him a big fly that seems to be tirelessly polishing its legs.

During the storm the light has dwindled, so much that now it is almost dark. All the day seems to have been swallowed by the river water, which glows now from within before the harbour lights come on.

IT'S NO USE TRYING TO EXPLAIN to American tourists why so many anachronistic cannons are aimed at them, here and there in the city. Raphaël talks about the fortifications that took a hundred years to build and have never been used. Ever since the English conquest, history has been filled with false alarms, and it makes a fine Tartarean desert, an awesome Syrtic shore for the soldiers at the Citadel perched high above. In their red coats and fur bonnets, they guard the beauty of the landscape and watch over the river and the clouds, awaiting a prodigious attack that has been delayed for two centuries now.

Sometimes Raphaël, the scrupulous guide, recalls that the birth of the city was a misunderstanding, the founders believing they were on the path to the Orient, with its wealth of gold and spices.

An ELONGATED FACE, HAIR smoothed down on either side of his hollow cheeks, eyes deep-set beneath the brow, and some vague powers that let him hold sway over a group of four boys and four girls. Since Eric left the church, all his attention in this base world is concentrated on seeking a secular moral code that will satisfy him and bring peace to his heart.

He has sworn that he will start afresh as if he had never lived. *To take eloquence and wring its neck* seems to have become the main concern of this former preaching brother. One thing only is necessary, he keeps telling himself. If he could just discover that primary necessity, all the rest would be organized around it, like a planet wrapping itself about its fiery nucleus. He thinks he has laid aside all principles and all his former ways of doing things. He imagines himself breathing like a newborn in the absolute new. Yet he has maintained an outmoded sense of charity that outstrips him and leads him where he doesn't want to go. He believes that the supreme virtue is to be detached from everything, come what may, yet compassion is still alive in him and it gives him no rest. He has not said to anyone, "Follow me and be perfect as my heavenly Father is perfect," but still they come after him and will not rest until he has told them how to become meek and lowly of heart. He has done nothing but talk to them about infinite peace and about the arbitrary nature of all power. His hoarse voice sometimes stumbles over words which he then retracts, confused. They listen and follow even his most stumbling utterance, so profound is the spell they are under, so urgent their desire for a new law. Where is life? they have been asking themselves for some time now, tired of the political intolerance in which their parents have brought them up. Hundreds of voices used to be raised in this city inhabited only by descendants of the founders, but now hearts are secretly questioning the propriety of living anywhere on the earth, that stretches as far as the eye can see, open and offered, without war or violence. What dream is this? they asked each other. To follow Eric they have abandoned father and mother, home, education and all certainty of being on this world's straight and narrow path. They have begun to grope, to search for peace with all their might. Sometimes Eric seemed to precede them along the path, sometimes he was very weary, even questioning his reason for living.

For a year now they have been sharing three rooms and a kitchen on rue Mont-Carmel.

They have pooled everything they possess, books, savings, jeans and T-shirts, sunflower seeds and millet, even their slender bodies, blithely changing partners according to the desire of the moment.

Eric likes to repeat that individual love, possessive passion, devastating jealousy, and all dual relationships must vanish from the peaceful city of their dreams.

A girl's high-pitched voice under a dark mass of curls states that Maud and Raphaël began very early to cheat, spending every night together.

They are all there, the friends of Maud and Raphaël, boys and girls on cushions or on the dark, varnished hardwood floor. They are meticulously shelling sunflower seeds, pecking at them in their palms.

They have offered Flora Fontanges a kitchen chair. She prefers to join them on the floor, using the chair as a back-rest, remaining a little off to one side, against the wall.

They begin talking among themselves, in low whining voices, talking about acid rain and the acid fog that is worse than the rain, then suddenly they fall silent as if they have exhausted any desire, any reason to speak.

The voice of the girl, under her dark mass of curly hair, rises again, addressing Flora Fontanges:

"I was the one who found Maud. At the airport in Lorette. She'd been there for three days, sleeping on a bench in her sleeping bag, wandering through the airport all day like a ghost. She asked me for a light. She was smoking Gauloises. She said she couldn't stay there because the police insisted she keep moving. I brought her to rue Mont-Carmel. She had a French accent."

Raphaël tells his story, as if he sees Maud in front of him, as if he's astounded to find her there.

"It was supper time. We squeezed together to make room for her. We all stopped eating to watch her eat. Like a starving dog. She wrapped her left arm around her plate as if she were protecting it from thieves. We'd never seen such hunger. She made all kinds of sounds with her mouth, her teeth, her throat. We were absolutely amazed. When she'd finished she pushed her plate away and started to cry and tremble from the cold."

Again, the girl with the strident voice:

"We all tried to comfort her and warm her with sweaters, scarves, hugs, but it was Raphaël who put her in his bed, under the blanket, and offered his pyjama top to sleep in."

"I kept her there in my bed for three nights. The first

night, she curled up against the wall and her whole body was shaken by sobs. The second night, she slept very peacefully, her hip brushing against me when she turned over. The third night she put her arms around my neck, cried for a while and kissed me on the neck."

Céleste continues grumpily, as if Maud's behaviour is again pushing her into heavy disapproval.

"The fourth night, I let her know that Raphaël wasn't the only available guy here. She didn't have to be asked twice to leave his bed. She soon picked another guy from the ones who were looking her over and the ones she'd been giving the eye to. She said 'François,' pointing at him, and he was kind of uncomfortable because he didn't know how to behave with her: she'd picked him so casually, as if it wasn't important. But the next night she was right back in Raphaël's bed."

Eric says the commune had been a great dream of his that had finally been realized, on rue Mont-Carmel.

Céleste points out that Raphaël and Maud almost caused the break-up of the commune. One fine night they went off to live together as a couple, like mom-and-dad in the olden days, back in the Dark Ages.

Céleste laughs, says the whole thing's fucking pathetic and reactionary.

Soon, Céleste confesses that she loves hanging out, just she and her sleeping bag, the search for a place to sleep being her daily problem, and that she only comes back to rue Mont-Carmel when she has no other choice. She points to the two silent boys who are standing next to Eric like unobtrusive acolytes and says there's not much choice since Raphaël left.

Flora Fontanges has been looking at the yellowed press clippings pinned to the wall of the small bedroom that opens off the kitchen.

Wanted. Maud, tall, slender, fair complexion, long black

hair, aged 13, wanted, no questions asked, her mother weeps, aged 15, 17, 18, no questions asked, her mother begs, long black hair, fair complexion, a runaway. Incomprehensible. She runs away. Can't help herself.

Miss Julie, painted face, blonde curly wig, whalebone collar, leg-o'mutton sleeves. Ah! how pretty the poster is, and see how completely Flora Fontanges, with all her pain and sorrow, disappears under the features of Julie wrangling with the valet.

Phaedra. A long white tunic with a Greek statue's rigid folds, eyes with false lashes and blue shadow, a hand on the breast feeling the pain of a heart that should never have been brought into this world.

The show must go on. Here is the frail heroine of *The Glass Menagerie* who moves as if she is broken, who grips our hearts. The tears are real, everything is real, the stomach pain, the urge to vomit. Wait for the end of the act. Come back for the bow. Six curtain calls. Radiant through her tears. Her real daughter disappeared three days ago.

The wheel turns. Everything is beginning again. This woman who was thought to have withdrawn from the world is back on stage. Flora Fontanges has returned to the city of her birth where she will play the part of Winnie in Samuel Beckett's *Happy Days*. The photograph resembles her, though she looks old and too made-up, with dark lips, delicate plucked eyebrows, bare brow, hair in broad waves breaking over her shoulders: a woman from another age. It is Raphaël who cut out the newspaper picture and stuck it on the wall.

He explains that Maud herself pinned up the other clippings. He has merely added one last "wanted" notice, written by him and never published, to come full circle, right beside the picture of Flora Fontanges advertising *Happy Days.*

Maud, aged twenty, faded jeans, white T-shirt, navy jacket, red sneakers, long black hair . . .

Flora Fontanges points out that the notice and the posters alternate neatly along the wall, as if their mutual dependence were obvious. As if it's clear that Maud vanishes into the dark every time her mother comes back on stage, to face the lights, the cheering audience . . .

She thinks: What a mess! and covers her face with her hands.

In the next room, Eric's halting voice says again that the notion of a worldwide fusion of brotherly love has always haunted him.

ONE WINTER DAY LONG AGO, when she had just arrived at the Eventurels on rue Bourlamaque, she was overcome by a startling thought that would not go away and threatened to plunge her into despair: that she would be no one but herself all her life, never able to change, that she would be Pierrette Paul forever, never escaping, confined within the same skin, tethered to the same heart, with no hope of change, just like that, with nothing ever happening, until old age and death. It was as if she could no longer move, as if both feet had sunk into the snow. Her breath formed a small curl of mist in the cold air.

People passed on the sidewalk beside her, walking quickly, faces red.

She was overcome by tremendous curiosity about these people she didn't know, by a strange attraction. How could she truly put herself in their places, understand what went on in their heads, in the most secret recesses of their lives? Suddenly she felt a great urge to become someone else, one of those passersby walking through the snow, for example. Her deepest desire was to live in some other place than within herself, for just a minute, one brief minute, to see what it is like inside a head other than her own, another body, to be incarnated anew, to know what it is like in some other place, to know new sorrows, new joys, to try on a different skin from her own, the way one tries on gloves in a store, to stop gnawing on the one bone of her actual life and feed on strange, disorienting substances. To shatter into ten, a hundred, a thousand indestructible fragments; to be ten, a hundred, a thousand new and indestructible persons. To go from one to the other, not lightly as one changes dresses, but to inhabit profoundly another being with all the knowledge, the compassion, the sense of rootedness, the efforts to adapt, and the strange and fearsome mystery that would entail.

She is standing, motionless, across from the apartment of M. and Mme Eventurel who have just adopted her. She has just recovered from a serious case of scarlet fever. She does not move but stands frozen there, half-buried in the snow, petrified at the thought of never being able to get out of herself.

All that happens long before rue Plessis. On rue Bourlamaque.

She does not yet know that one day she will become an actress and will break her heart into a thousand pieces as brilliant as suns.

The grey sky is low enough to touch with a finger, on the rim of the horizon. A small girl muffled like a roly-poly is standing in the snow at twilight, outside the door of 101, rue Bourlamaque. This is the winter hour, the saddest hour of all. Twilight. Dusk. The hour before night. When day has already withdrawn. The wan light given off by the snow as far as the eye can see, like a muted lantern. This small quantity of day at ground level exhales its cold breath, half-swallowed by the snow.

She dreams of having access to the sun and to the night, of learning how the light progresses, at the risk of burning herself therein.

Someone calls to her from the window, scarcely ajar because of the cold. They name her Marie Eventurel. It is a new name, pure product of the imagination of a barren old couple who yearn for a child. Now she need only answer to the name that she's been given and say yes, that's me, my name is Marie Eventurel, I'll do whatever you tell me, I'll be the person you want me to be, as you wish me to be, until my longing to be another person takes over, pushing me and pulling me far from you and the city, across the sea, where I shall be an actress, in the old country.

The day will come when she will choose her own name, and it will be the secret name, hidden in her heart since the dawn of time, the one and only name that will designate her among all others, and allow her all the metamorphoses needed for her life.

If you aren't careful the child could freeze to death. Flora Fontanges can do nothing for the little girl in the snow. Except take responsibility for the tingling and burning of her cold-numbed fingers and toes as soon as she enters the Eventurels' overheated apartment.

For the brief time she is there, Flora Fontanges runs the risk of seeing Madame Eventurel herself, her little black velvet hat, her veil, her straight back, her solemn slowness, while the apartment on rue Bourlamaque will open up under her footsteps, with its small dark bedrooms and long corridor.

Here was the start of everything in her life with M. and Mme Eventurel.

"Come on, Raphaël, let's go!"

Everything goes to wrack and ruin, the house of blackened bricks, the outside wooden staircases and most of all, the gaping opening to the basement, dug below street level, a shadowy hole in which no doubt is hidden the ghost of Monsieur Eventurel in his steel grey suit with white stripes, infinitely dignified, despite bankruptcy and seizure.

Flora Fontanges has nothing more to do on rue Bourlamaque, she quickens her pace and pulls Raphaël along by his arm.

At TIMES A SORT OF FEVERISH anticipation appears on Raphaël's face from looking at her so hard, when he is no longer altogether sure of what he's saying, caught unprepared, waiting for her to ask the questions, to answer them herself. Suddenly, he hopes for everything from her. Absolute revelation. Is she not in the fullness of her womanhood, an accomplished individual for whom love and the pain of love have no secrets?

Raphaël's beauty, his profound and untouched youth, his look of enchantment when he recites a poem.

I am the child you love to sing to sleep.

They are both alone in Eric's apartment. She, on the chair that is intended for her; he, kneeling at her feet. He buries his face in the folds of Flora Fontanges's skirt, complains he's been dying of loneliness since Maud's gone away.

She takes Raphaël's head in her hands, her long slender fingers graze the forehead, the soft eyelids, the slender bridge of the nose, the damp mouth, the smooth cheeks pierced by a surprisingly rough young beard.

For a moment he shuts his eyes between her hands, surrendering himself like a cat. Then leaps to his feet. Pleads with her:

50

"Please, Madame Fontanges, you can do better than that, you can console me like a real woman who fears neither God nor the devil. Like a real mother endlessly bringing new life into the world, generous in forgiving. Take me with you tonight to the hotel, I beg you. I don't want to sleep alone and I don't want Céleste in my bed."

Flora Fontanges says that she fears neither God nor the devil and that she's not sure she has ever been a real mother. Only the streets of the city frighten her and perhaps, too, the sorrows of others when she can do nothing to console them.

"You're tough, Madame Fontanges, but I can get along very well without you, you know . . ."

"That's too bad for you, Raphaël dear, and too bad for me."

They walked together through the summer night, along fragrant streets murmuring with life. He began very soon to look around him, noticing all sorts of charming and amusing things in the city, so that when they reached the hotel on rue Sainte-Anne he seemed altogether comforted and happy.

He fell asleep almost at once, fully clothed, on one of the twin beds, while Flora Fontanges watched over him in the dark, as one watches over a sick child.

Raphaël's finely delineated features persist in the room, where all the lights have been extinguished. Her fingers preserve the memory of them, as if she were blind.

SHE DISLIKES BEING WATCHED BY the director. Gilles Perrault's blue eyes through his little round glasses make her think of his resemblance to an old owl. However, in reality this man, apparently innocuous and bland, is a fierce hunter lying in wait for whatever will claw, bite, damage the soul and body of Flora Fontanges. Ever since he started dreaming about an emaciated Winnie, confined to her sand-pile, slowly suffocated grain by grain, facing an enraptured audience. A small corrida for an old woman whose death never ends.

He insists that she go on a diet, even though she is already very slender and tall. He rubs his hands. He will wait as long as necessary for the degeneration of Flora Fontanges to occur. He wants her to be as brittle as glass, to be gravely wounded and totally submissive to old age and death. He grants her one final extension before the first reading. All that matters now is July fifteenth. Once again he looks defiantly into her face. The myopic's single-minded insistence. He cracks his knuckles. Swallows.

Flora Fontanges promises herself not to touch the script of *Happy Days* before July fifteenth. Vows that she will enjoy her pathetic freedom until July fifteenth. The first reading will be unsullied for her. She will probably stammer as she faces her partner, grope in the dark of her own soul for the fleeting soul of Winnie. In the meantime she will let Raphaël, Eric, or Céleste keep her company, their radiant youth surrounding her, a kind of feast.

There will always be time for Flora Fontanges to offer up her spirit on the stage, just once more, until death ensues.

Eric SAYS STRANGE THINGS. IN HIS mouth words are urgent, they jostle and clash, inaudible, evasive, they explode, then silence briefly falls and they break out again, brutal and sharp. You could believe that voices other than his are seeking an outlet on his tongue and in his mouth. He is saddled with incoherent voices. He never knows exactly what is being spoken by his lips. Sometimes he thinks he is alone within himself. For a moment, he breathes and is appeased. Then it all begins again. Eric is haunted by the living and the dead. The whole city, starting with his closest relatives, seems to have chosen him as a spokesman. Some voices call for absolute love, others for money pure and simple, all complain that earthly goods are insufficient though they look fine, a broken voice is heard among the others talking about the promise, never kept, of eternal life. The voice is that of Sister Eulalie-de-Dieu, a distant cousin of Eric's who died at twenty-three, at the Hôtel-Dieu, speaking out of the heart of death.

His head slumps to his chest, his hair plastered down incredibly smoothly and falling on either side, making him look like a drowned man. He says we must return to the source of the earth, back to our original brotherhood with plants and animals, stop believing in the arrogant separation of woman and man from the rest of creation.

"All evil stems from the pretentious invention of the soul that's been reserved for human beings. Either this mysterious soul doesn't exist at all or it is incarnate everywhere, rudimentary or complex depending on the bodies, the splendid terrestrial bodies. The same breath of life, the same energy, makes a leaf stir in the wind, creates a small pink shrimp or a nervous and sensitive cat, and creates the man and woman who study the mysteries of life."

Eric hears scraps of conversation. The everyday words of his parents come back to him, greedy and stupid. Speculation, markets, real estate, selling, buying . . . Eric refused his legacy when his parents died in a car accident. He took a vow of poverty in the secrecy of his heart. He fidgets, stammers, talks about business offices and banks— dens of iniquity.

Eric's incoherence bothers no one; an obscure thread at the very root of his being seems to link his muddled words. Eric wonders about the inhabitants of the city just as persistently as his parents used to keep an eye on real estate fluctuations. The living and the dead cry out in him with broken voices.

"If I get to sign that contract, I'll go crazy with joy. This time, it'll be the salvation of me."

What can he do about his mother's final words? If it's true that she had no time to sign the hoped-for contract, did she see in a flash the blind face of her salvation before death burned her eyes? And what kind of salvation is there when the body no longer exists, is a blazing torch amid the twisted metal of an automobile in flames?

Eric keeps repeating that the only good poverty is voluntary, that the other kind, the kind that is imposed and causes pain, is criminal and destructive. Sometimes when he and his friends are together, he denounces the poverty

petty

of little Claire Lagueux, who was crooked and bent because she never slept in a real bed of the proper size, but in a deal box set on the kitchen floor, until she was five.

Eric thinks that knowledge and learning must pass first through the body. He has only pity for those students who live in an ivory tower, retreat their only way of dwelling in the world.

"I have chosen you and you have chosen me. Together we shall possess the earth."

All these boys and girls around him have trained themselves to be patient through manual tasks. They are attentive to their five senses, cultivating them as if they were miracles. To tell hot from cold, to experience dry and wet, bitter and salt, smooth and rough, to learn how muscular effort bears and supports the weight of things, to breathe the smell of the city, grasp the passage of light on the river, communicate directly with the earth, to have no car or motor-scooter, to travel through the city step by step, at the rhythm of one's heart, to study the earth with one's entire body, like a small child discovering the world.

They set themselves to work at it courageously, giving up their parents' money and often their education, which depends on money. Sometimes, at night, before they fall into a heavy sleep, they listen to their aching bodies vibrate with the accumulated experience of the day. What they hear is like a harsh and pungent song as the whole body gives over its secrets, which the heart can hear distinctly in the night.

To rediscover the initial poverty, the first freshness of all sensations, with no recollection or known reference. The taste of the world at its birth. What dream is it that makes Eric live in his gentle madness?

They wash stacks of plates in restaurant kitchens, peel tons of potatoes, drive horses and calèches crammed with tourists gobbling chips and popcorn, pick strawberries on the Ile d'Orléans and peaches in the Niagara Valley, they deposit their cash in the kitty established for that purpose, and they eat like squirrels.

Céleste and Raphaël escape now and then, long enough for a good restaurant meal which they talk about afterwards, with delectation, after they've repaid the common cashbox.

Eric presses his face against the window which glistens with rain. The whole city is there, half-hidden by its old sick elms, a few skyscrapers emerging from the close-packed mass of houses. Eric listens to the song of the rain as if he can hear a mass of little voices telling him about the city, secretly, in the night.

STREETS, LANES, PUBLIC SQUARES: Raphaël has started to peel away all the lives of the city, century by century, as if stripping layers of wallpaper. A historian's job, he thinks, not wanting to be like Eric, with his nostalgia for a lost paradise.

Raphaël wants Flora Fontanges to accompany him on his search.

"I'm going to awaken the past, bring out characters still alive, buried under the debris. I'll give them to you to see and to hear. I'll write historical plays for you. You'll play all the women and you'll be enthralling as never before. You'll see."

They scour the city from top to bottom and from bottom to top, they follow the irregularities of the cape in successive stages, from the Citadel to Les Foulons.

Here, there are only hills. Generations of horses have broken their backs on them. The girls have dancers' calves. Exhausted hearts. Côte du Palais, Côte de la Montagne, Côte de la Fabrique, Côte de la Négresse, Côte à Coton, Sainte-Ursule, Sainte-Angèle, Stanislas, Lachevrotière, Saint-Augustin . . .

These abrupt names have long haunted Flora Fontanges, a strange jumble, touching her suddenly, without warning, in the foreign countries where she was an actress, sometimes at night on her way back to the hotel after the performance, or in a restaurant in the middle of a meal, around the table with the cast after a few bottles, when a last toast was being drunk in honour of someone who had no name, when they suddenly ran short of imagination and could think of no one in whose honour to clink glasses. Flora Fontanges would raise her glass. *Salut*, she would say, Côte à Coton, des Grisons, Stanislas or Sainte-Ursule, and no one knew what she was talking about.

"The most wonderful thing," said Raphaël, "is that if you turn around after you've been climbing, you can see the mountain in the distance, and the open sky above the valley."

A thousand days had passed, and a thousand nights, and there was forest, another thousand days and thousand nights, and there was still the forest, great sweeps of pine and oak hurtling down the headland to the river, and the mountain was behind, low and squat, one of the oldest on the globe, and it was covered with trees as well. There was an unending accumulation of days and nights in the wildness of the earth.

"Only pay attention," said Raphaël, "and you can feel on your neck, on your shoulders, the extraordinary coolness of countless trees, while a roar, loud yet muffled, rises from the forest deep as the sea. The earth is soft and sandy under our feet, covered with moss and dead leaves."

Is it so difficult then to make a garden in the middle of the forest, and to surround it with a palisade like a treasure-trove? The first man was called Louis Hébert, the first woman Marie Rollet. They sowed the first garden with seeds that came from France. They laid out the garden according to the notion of a garden, the memory of a garden, that they carried in their heads, and it was almost indistinguishable from a garden in France, flung into a forest in the New World. Carrots, lettuces, leeks, cabbages, all in a straight line, in serried ranks along a taut cord, amid the wild earth all around. When the apple tree brought here from Acadia by Monsieur de Mons and transplanted finally yielded its fruit, it became the first of all the gardens in the world, with Adam and Eve standing before the Tree. The whole history of the world was starting afresh because of a man and a woman planted in this new earth.

One night, unable to sleep because of the mosquitoes, they went outside together. They looked at the night and at the shadow of Cape Diamond which is blacker than night. They realize they are not looking at the same sky. Even the sky is different here, with a new arrangement of the stars and the familiar signs. Where are the Big Dipper and Canis Major and Canis Minor, Betelgeuse, and Capella? The sky above their heads has been transformed like the earth beneath their feet. Above, below, the world is no longer the same because of the distance that exists between this world and the other, the one that was once theirs and never will be theirs again. Life will never again be the same. Here in this night is their new life, with its rough breathing, its sharp air never before inhaled. They are with that life, they are caught in it like little fish in black water.

The children and grandchildren in their turn remade the gardens in the image of the first one, using seeds that the new earth had yielded. Little by little, as generations passed, the mother image has been erased from their memories. They have arranged the gardens to match their own ideas and to match the idea of the country they come more and more to resemble. They have done the same with churches, and with houses in town and in the country. The secret of the churches and houses has been lost along the way. They began floundering as they built houses of God and their own dwellings. The English came, and the Scots, and the Irish. They had their own ideas and images for houses, stores, streets, and public squares, while the space for gardens receded into the countryside. The city itself laid out, more and more sharply defined, more precise, with streets of beaten earth racing against each other up and down the cape.

Flora Fontanges is struck by the early days of the city as Raphaël evokes them. He becomes animated. Thinks that the old life is there waiting to be recaptured in all its freshness, thanks to history. She says that time recaptured is theatre, and that she is prepared to play Marie Rollet then and there.

"A headdress from the Ile de France, a blue twill apron with a bib, earth under my nails because of the garden, and there is Eve who has just arrived with Adam, the King's apothecary. And Adam, Raphaël dear, is you."

She laughs. Shuts her eyes. She is an actress inventing a role for herself. She manages the passage from her life today to a life of the past. She appropriates the heart, the loins, the hands of Marie Rollet. Seeks the light of her gaze. She opens her eyes. Smiles at Raphaël.

"Am I a good likeness, Raphaël dear?"

He asserts that the creation of the world was very near here, and that it is easy to go back to the first days of the earth.

She goes through the motions of adjusting an imaginary headdress on her short hair. She has been transfigured, from head to foot. At once rejuvenated and weightier. Laden with a mysterious mission. She is the mother of the country. For a moment. A brief moment. Before declaring:

"That's all mimicry. I'm a chameleon, Raphaël dear, and it's terribly tiring."

Suddenly she goes numb, like someone regaining her foothold in everyday life. She wants to go home. Says again that she's very tired. An ordinary woman now, lacklustre, on her son's arm, walking through the city streets.

That evening, Céleste assumed an injured look and declared that this whole story Raphaël and Flora Fontanges had made up about the city's founders was phoney and slanted.

"The first man and the first woman in this country had copper-coloured skin and wore feathers in their hair. As for the first garden, there was no beginning or end, just a tangled mass of corn and potatoes. The first human gaze that lit on the world was the gaze of an Amerindian, and that was how he saw the Whites coming down the river, on big ships rigged out with white sails and crammed with rifles and cannons, with holy water and fire water."

For a long time Flora Fontanges has been a stealer of souls, in hospitals, asylums, the street, salons, backstage. She would lie in wait for the dying or those in sound health, for the innocent and the mad, for ordinary people and for others full of pretensions, for those who are masked and those who go through life exposed, their faces bare as hands, for those without love and others who are radiant with overflowing passion, like monstrances.

She takes from them their gestures and their tics, the way they bend their heads and lower their eyes, and she feeds on their blood and their tears. She learns how to live and how to die. She has models who are alive, and the dead laid out on their hospital beds. How long has she spent at the bedsides of the dying, spying on their last breath, on the supreme moment when the features stiffen and all at once go white, like old bones? She has held the little mirror to dying mouths, thinking to see the soul's passing in the mist that forms, wanting to take hold of that evanescent soul and give to it an additional life, wanting to use it this very night when she plays *Camille*.

And Raphaël? Perhaps he has no soul. All that she can

be sure about him is his strange beauty, utterly animal and disconcerting. Is it possible that he has no mystery or any hidden dream, like smooth water? Here there is nothing for Flora Fontanges, who is a thief, to steal. Raphaël eludes her, like innocence.

That night, Flora Fontanges had a dream. Her daughter Maud appeared to her, her long black freshly combed hair framing her face, falling to her shoulders and her chest, gliding from her waist to her hips. Maud talked with her mouth shut, her lips unmoving, with no line stirring on her very white face. Maud's voice was audible as if from far away, behind a wall of ice. She declared that Raphaël had the name of an archangel and the teeth of a wolf. At that moment Raphaël's dazzling smile filled all the space in Flora Fontanges's dream, erasing the image of Maud at one stroke. His smile, like the Cheshire cat's, floated in the still air, while Raphaël's face and body remained hidden. Then little by little his smile disappeared, like a drawing under an eraser. It began to turn very dark and very cold in Flora Fontanges's dream.

O NE CLIMBS UP AND DOWN IN
the city, one sees the mountain, then no longer sees it.
The layout of the streets is unpredictable. Her past life
and her present life also lie in wait for everything that
passes, like a small wild animal alert for its prey. Flora
Fontanges listens to Raphaël's stories, draws from them
characters and roles. Sometimes she can see clearly before
her the women Raphaël has conjured up, dressed in the
finery of a bygone age. She breathes the breath of life
into their nostrils and begins to live fully in their place.
Is enchanted by this power she possesses.

At the residence of Monsieur le Gouverneur they ape the
court of the King of France. The men have curly wigs and
hats with plumes, the women, tall fluted headdresses of
muslin and lace. There is wrangling over precedences and
privileges in a residence from which the bark has just
been stripped. While all around comes the growl of the
forest's green and resinous breath, sometimes advancing
by night like an army on the march, threatening at any
moment to encircle us, to close in on us and take us for
its own.

The governor's daughter is twelve years old; she turns

in her bed, inhales through the walls the forest's vast breath. The howling of wolves mingles with the wild smell of the earth. The governor's daughter is overcome by nightmares and dread. Says she wants to go back to France. Her father reprimands her, complaining that she is not brave, promising she will be married soon, to an officer of the Carignan regiment.

The governor's daughter has blonde hair, and she is slender and tall. She dances a ravishing minuet. When night falls her eyes are dilated by fear.

They have named her Angélique.

For a moment Flora Fontanges tries on at her wrists the chilly little hands of the governor's daughter. She feels a morbid fear. Frees herself at once to join Raphaël, who is waiting for her at the door to the General Hospital.

THEY ARE THERE, BOTH OF THEM, amid the disorientation of the convent and of time, heedful of what role the life of the past might be playing in this closely guarded place.

On the wall, three young sisters painted by Plamondon testify to their earthly monastic existence, even though they have long since been merely ashes and dust. They persist in a *tableau vivant* as a witness, captured for all time by the eyes of a painter who apprehended them and followed them to the threshold of the mystery, before he too fell silent and vanished into dust.

In a glass showcase, among the pious souvenirs on display there, are a little wrought-iron hammer and scissors, the work of a nun who died in 1683, according to the Sister who guards the museum.

Raphaël and Flora Fontanges must awaken a little nun, faceless and nameless, and keep her alive beneath their gaze, long enough to imagine her story.

Please God, thinks Flora Fontanges, let me be clairvoyant again, let me see with my eyes, hear with my ears, let me suffer a thousand deaths and a thousand pleasures with all my body and all my soul, let me be another woman again. This time, it is a nun at the General Hospital, and

I shall remake her life from the beginning.

"It's quite an accomplishment to go back in time and draw their secrets from the dead," Raphaël murmurs in Flora Fontanges's ear.

Once again they agree, perfect accomplices in a game that enchants them. They wish and are able to summon the past to the city, to restore the light and colour to the air that covered everything when the city was merely a village tucked away between river and forest. Now it is a matter of reviving a faded sun, of replacing it in the sky like a ball of light: is that so difficult, after all?

The high tide spreads itself from shore to shore; one can hear it lapping gently against the wharfs when the forge is still and the flame stands briefly erect and motionless. A girl wearing a leather apron that falls to her feet is doing a boy's job at her father's forge on rue Saint-Paul. Standing in the heat and glare of the fire, she wields the forge, the hammer, and the tongs, she pounds the iron, gleaming and streaming with sweat, then takes it from the furnace to the basin of cool water in which she plunges her work. The flame is no longer on her face and she is all black in the dark. Her father, arms folded, watches with admiration as she works, and his heart is heavy, for his daughter must leave him soon to enter the convent.

For a long time she has been childlike and good, the delight of her father and stepmother. Then, at the table one day, she declared before everyone that she wanted to become a blacksmith like her father. There were no boys in the family. Six daughters from the first marriage, like a garden in which all the flowers are blue, without the shadow of another color. She wrote with a black pencil on a sheet of white paper, in highly wrought and ornate letters: THIBAULT AND DAUGHTER, BLACKSMITHS. You could see at once that it would make a very pretty sign. The father smiled, quite dazed, and overcome by uncertainty and doubt. The stepmother shrieked that she must be possessed by the devil to be thinking of such a thing. She talked of bringing in the exorcist.

A tall girl with broad shoulders, a sweet face, and strong hands effortlessly lifts heavy weights, and she smiles almost all the time. Guillemette Thibault is a fine name, one to bear all one's life, never to change for the name of some stranger who would take her as his wife. She has already refused two suitors and she wants to take over from her father at the forge. Everyone has joined in to reason with her, the stepmother first, then her five sisters and the curé. The father is silent and lowers his head.

She listens to them, her face leaning into the shadow of her coif, her sturdy hands flat on her knees. What she is hearing now has been told her time and time again. There is men's work and women's work, and the world is in order. Marriage or the convent: for a girl there's no other way out. She looks at her hands on her knees, she listens to her heart beat in her chest, and it's as if all the strength and the joy in her heart and in her hands were freezing inch by inch.

Guillemette Thibault decided in favour of the convent. But before she entered the convent her father allowed her to forge on the anvil and in the fire a pair of scissors and a little hammer, so delicate and finely made that she brought them along to the General Hospital with her trousseau and her dowry, as an offering.

What she feared most in the world, that her name be taken from her, subsequently came to pass. After two years of novitiate, she became Sister Agnès-de-la-Pitié and no one ever heard of Guillemette Thibault again.

THEY LIKE WALKING IN THE PORT
at the end of the day, when a warm mist rises from the
water, and sky, earth and water, ships, wharfs, docks, sailors
and strollers, are mingled, mixed, confused in a single
white and hazy substance.

So much looking at the river has given her a vacant
stare; she can no longer sort out her images, but lets
herself be assailed by all that passes, then passes again,
near and far, on the water and in the harbour and even
in her memory.

He feels like waving his hand in front of Flora Fontanges's
eyes to bring her back to him, make her stop staring into
space.

"Flora, what is it you see that I don't?"

He has never before used her Christian name and he
struggles to meet her gaze. The water hovers, as far as
the eye can see. Small waves pound the pier, oily filaments
congeal at the edge and glimmer gold and violet.

She stretches her arms towards the watery void.

"Out there, the *Empress of Britain*, moored at pier 21!"

Her voice changes. She appears to be speaking to no
one, inclines her head as if fascinated. All that seems to
matter to her now is the brownish water close against the

pier, with its greasy traces of oil. The horizon is blocked, she thinks. The breadth and majesty of the river prove to be obstructed by the massive white bulk of the *Empress of Britain*. Flora Fontanges has nothing to look at now but the expanse of dirty water between the pier and the liner, which spreads before her eyes as the *Empress* wrenches herself from the earth, in long oily trails.

Is it her greatest fear that her true face will suddenly loom into view and appear before her, mingling with the huddled crowd that is leaning on the rails? The broad waves of her hair falling to her shoulders, her small face as it was before all the masks of the theatre, hard as a stone, her gaze fixed obstinately on the water, between the pier and the boat. While on the pier crowded with people waving handkerchiefs and shouting inaudibly into the wind, perhaps M. and Mme Eventurel will appear, both of them tall and thin in their dark clothes: Madame's white face speckled with black by her thick veil, Monsieur's silhouette tightly buttoned into a velvet-collared black coat.

If M. and Mme Eventurel were to show themselves again to Flora Fontanges, she would see that they are deeply offended and angry with her for all eternity, motionless and congealed in their resentment, and that she just has to disappear again now, as she did in 1937, on the *Empress of Britain*.

She says "Good Lord" and buries her face in her hands.

She cannot, however, stop a thin young girl in a severely tailored grey suit from haunting her memory, from making the same movements as in 1937, from experiencing again the same fever and the same guilty joy at the mere thought of leaving M. and Mme Eventurel, of crossing the ocean and becoming an actress in the face of all opposition.

In the time it takes the Eventurels' adopted daughter to slip on the black dress, the embroidered apron and the flimsy headdress of the *Empress of Britain* chambermaids, the piers have disappeared altogether, far behind the wake of the ship. M. and Mme Eventurel have already toppled onto the horizon. Forever.

"I went away on the *Empress of Britain* and never came back."

He has stopped paying attention to what she says. He is following his own thoughts, looking out straight ahead, at the river covered with mist, studying the passage of his own moving images, evoking them himself, giving them their proper life and form as they appear, as if he were preparing a history lesson with slides.

"Let's go now, Raphaël dear! There's nothing more to see here."

He says you can look at the river and question the horizon forever.

ALWAYS, PEOPLE HAVE DONE THEIR utmost to see as far as they can, as if they might be able to extend their gaze to the gulf and surprise the ocean at her source, as it begins coming near us for our happiness or our despair. In winter, nothing comes at all because of the ice, and the waiting for spring is interminable.

In the winter of 1759, after the battle of Sainte-Foy had been won, they reached an agreement with the English occupier that lasted a few months, with the hope of seeing the arrival that spring of French ships laden with arms and munitions, with provisions and blue-uniformed soldiers. Never has the breakup of the ice, shattering and jamming, never has the cawing of the first crow after a winter without birds, been more eagerly awaited. But when at last the surface of the water started moving again, driven by an unseen force, it was English vessels that were making their way along the river, numerous and in orderly fashion. France had ceded us to England like a burden to be shed. What happened to us then, suddenly, like an ill wind, was almost indistinguishable from utter despair.

Raphaël talks about a bygone time, long before the English conquest, at the very beginning of the world, when every step that was taken upon the naked earth was wrenched from the brush and the forest.

They are all there on the shore, waiting for the ships from France. Governor, Intendant and gentlemen in their Sunday best, bedecked, beplumed and covered with frills and furbelows, in spite of the heat and mosquitoes. A few nuns resist the wind as best they can amid a great stirring of veils, of wimples, scapulars, cornets, and neckcloths. Newly disbanded soldiers, freshly shaven, following orders, wearing clean shirts, eyes open so wide that the sun looks red to them, waiting for the promise that is marching towards them along the vast river that shimmers in the sun.

Below, at the top of the cape, is the sketch of a city planted in the wildness of the earth, close against the breath of the forest, filled with the cries of birds and muffled stirrings in the suffocating heat of July.

This time it's not just flour and sugar, rabbits, roosters, and hens, cows and horses, pewter jugs and horn-handled knives, lengths of wool and muslin, tools and cheese-cloth:

this is a cargo of marriageable girls, suited for reproduction, which is the matter at hand.

New France has a bad reputation in the mother country. People speak of a "place of horror" and of the "suburbs of hell." Peasant women need coaxing. They have to turn to the Salpêtrière, that home for former prostitutes, to populate the colony.

Now they are crowded here onto the bridge, huddled together like a bouquet too tightly bound. The wings of their headdresses beat in the wind and they wave handkerchiefs above their heads. The men, in ranks on the shore, stare at them silently. The decency of their costumes has been observed, at once and with satisfaction, by the Governor and the Intendant. Now they must find out, even before the women's faces can be distinguished, whether they are modest and their persons carefully tended. The rest of the meticulous, precise examination will be carried out at the proper time and place, little by little, even as they make their way towards us with their young bodies dedicated unreservedly to man, to work, and to motherhood.

In the absence of peasant women, they must now be content with these persons of no account who have come from Paris, with a dowry from the King of fifty *livres* per head. Though they already know how to sew, knit, and make lace (this they have been taught at the Salpêtrière, "a place as ignominious as the Bastille"), we'll just see the looks on their faces when they have to help the cow to calve and change its litter.

Now their features can be seen clearly in the light, framed with white linen and wisps of hair in the wind. Some are red and tanned by the sun and the sea air, others are bloodless and skeletal, consumed by seasickness and fear.

The men stand on the shore, on this splendid day, as if they were seeing the northern lights. Now and then cries burst from their heaving chests.

"Ah! the pretty redhead! That lovely one in blue! The little one with curls!"

When men have been without women for so long, save for a few squaws, it's a pleasure to see such a fine collection of petticoats and rumpled linen coming toward us. It has been arranged, between Monsieur the Governor, Monsieur the Intendant, and ourselves, the marriageable boys, that we would take them as they are, these *filles du Roi*, fresh and young and without a past, purified by the sea during a long rough crossing on a sailing ship. Thirty passengers died along the way and had to be cast overboard like stones. The survivors will long be haunted by the lurching and pitching, so deeply does the ocean's great flux still inhabit their bodies, from the roots of their hair to the tips of their toes. They are like a procession of drunken girls as they make their way to us along the gangplank. Their lovely shoulders straining under shawls crossed on their breasts sway like sailors on a spree.

Monsieur the Intendant is categorical. *All discharged soldiers, some of them dealing as brigands, will be barred from fur-trading and hunting and the honours of the Church and the religious communities if, within a fortnight after the arrival of the* filles du Roi, *they have not married.*

The fattest ones were chosen first, during brief visits in the house lent for that purpose by Madame de la Peltrie. It is better that they be plump, to resist the rigours of the climate, so they say, and besides, when you've consumed misery through all the pores of your skin in the King's armies for years, it is comforting to sink your teeth into a good solid morsel, for the time God grants us in this land that has been a barren waste since the creation of the world. In reality, only hunting and fishing are possible here. The condition of *coureur de bois* would suit us well enough, although it is the King's will that we be fettered to a piece of land covered with standing timber, with a woman who talks on and on, claiming that she has emerged from between our ribs to take her first breath here, in the earthly paradise. What answer is there, then, to that expectation, that desire for absolute love which torments most of the women? Only the succession of days and nights will win out over their fine ardour. That's because it wears you down in the end, to withstand the fire of summer, the fire of winter, the same intolerable burning from which the only escape is a wooden shack fifteen feet square, covered with straw. In the dwelling's only bed we take each other, and then again, and give birth and accumulate children, it is where we spend our dying days, then breathe our last. Sometimes it resembles a pigsty, and tears mingle with sperm and sweat, while generations pass and life constantly remakes itself, like the air we breathe.

garden of Eden,
new world

STANDING ON THE PIER AT ANSE aux Foulons, surrounded by the smell of tar and the falling night, Raphaël and Flora Fontanges have started to recite the names of the King's girls, the *filles du Roi*, like a litany of saints, names hidden away in dusty archives forever.

Graton, Mathurine
Gruau, Jeanne
Guerrière, Marie-Bonne
Hallier, Perette
d'Orange, Barbe
Drouet, Catherine
de la Fitte, Apolline
Doigt, Ambroisine
Jouanne, Angélique
La Fleur, Jacobine
Le Seigneur, Anne
Salé, Elisabeth
Deschamps, Marie

In reality, it concerns her alone, the queen with a thousand names, the first flower, first root, Eve in person (no longer embodied solely by Marie Rollet, wife of Louis

Hébert), but fragmented now into a thousand fresh faces, Eve in her manifold greenness, her fertile womb, her utter poverty, endowed by the King of France in order to found a country, who is exhumed and emerges from the bowels of the earth. Green branches emerge from between her thighs, an entire tree filled with birdsong and tender leaves, coming to us and casting shade from river to mountain, from mountain to river, and we are in the world like children struck with awe.

One day our mother Eve embarked on a great sailing ship, travelled across the ocean for long months, making her way to us who did not yet exist, to bring us out of nothing, out of the scent of a barren land. In turn blonde, brunette, or auburn, laughing and crying at once, it is she, our mother, who gives birth in the fullness of life, mingled with the seasons, with earth and dung, with snow and frost, fear and courage, her rough hands running over our faces, scraping our cheeks, and we are her children.

At the end of a long chain of life begun three centuries ago, Raphaël and Flora Fontanges look at one another as if self-conscious at being there, both of them, facing one another, in the month of July 1976, with their hands and their arms, their feet and their legs, their astonished faces, their hidden sex, their separate stories, their respective ages.

Let the *filles du Roi* be reduced to dust, thinks Flora Fontanges, let the dead bury the dead. It is pointless to search among the mothers of this country for the mother she has never known. Orphaned from her first cry and first breath, Flora Fontanges has no business here among the *filles du Roi*, revived through the imagination of a history student and of an old woman who has been bereft of her own mother from the dawn of time.

And if life were only that? The notion of absolute maternal goodness, just like that, at the end of the world, and you set out to meet it, directing your life towards it, anyone, anywhere, anyhow, so strong are both hope and desire, all of us are like that, like someone who does not truly see, an orphan without hearth or home, while our blind fingers move mistakenly across the soft and tender face of love. It's using a carrot to make the world move like the donkey in the fable. So many disappointing loves for Flora Fontanges and always the same hope renascent from the ashes when the furtive face of love withdraws. How strange is the life that she leads, and how difficult love is to grasp! What is the initial wound of love, for everyone, not just for Flora Fontanges who has no father or mother? What was it for Maud who has been loved desperately since birth, who has been a runaway from birth, who is constantly running away, straight ahead, not looking back, as if life existed somewhere in the distance, hidden in the clouds?

His barely audible voice, the pause between his words, that lost look of his.

"What if Maud's gone away with someone else?"

In the end they seek reasons for Maud's departure, they imagine responsibilities, feel guilt, a sort of vague complicity.

He lifts his grave and childlike face towards her:

"Why did she go away? Is it my fault? Yours?"

What is this loss? There is always someone who's not there when you need him. How to accept that without fretting, without trying with all one's might to avoid its ever happening: this absence, this negligence of the heart?

"And Maud was so secretive, so inaccessible. Who could know?"

"I never asked her any questions. I liked her to be secretive and inaccessible, so beautiful and untouched inside her mystery, alone with me as if she were alone with herself, with no secrets. And then she went away, just

when I couldn't get along without her, without her mystery
and her smooth face and her eyes that were open too
wide. I think she sensed that, and she was afraid I'd close
her up inside a stifling intimacy . . ."

"If love is a trap, it was different with me, it was just
the opposite. There were many dropped stitches in the
net, there was nothing to hold her back and she couldn't
bear that. An actress mother isn't the easiest thing for a
child. Too much cuddling at one time, between two per-
formances, then long absences when I was on tour. It's
not normal, alternating between too much and nothing.
Impossible to live with, very likely."

They both reach the same conclusion. For different,
sometimes contrary reasons, at a certain point Maud in-
evitably finds herself facing the intolerable, and then she
can only run away.

"If she comes back it won't be the same. I won't be
able to live quietly as we did before. I'd be too afraid
she'd go away again. I'd probably start asking her questions,
pestering her about her escapades, about her past, both
recent and remote. I don't think I'll be able to accept
her secrecy any more. I might even become jealous and
wicked like everyone else . . ."

That sulky pout, the tear on the rim of the lashes.
Raphaël repeats that he is wicked, jealous, jealous, and
says it's destroying him.

The boy slumps suddenly as if his whole life is a burden.

Flora Fontanges squeezes in her hand the long strong
hand that rests flat on the table. She says that Maud will
come back. Maud always comes back. She talks to him as
if he were an old close friend. She feels light and experienced in grace, a kind, consoling woman at the side of
a weeping child.

Raphaël starts to talk animatedly again about the *filles
du Roi*, as if his life depended on it.

THEY MUST ALL OF THEM BE named aloud, all of them called by their names, while we face the river whence they emerged in the seventeenth century, to give birth to us and to a country.

Michel, Jaquette
Mignolet, Gillette
Moullard, Eléonore
Palin, Claude-Philiberte
Le Merle d'Aupré, Marguerite

It is nothing for Flora Fontanges and Raphaël to recite a rosary of girls' names, to pay homage to them, greet them as they pass, to bring them onto the shore—their light ashes—to have them become flesh again, just long enough for a friendly greeting. All, without exception: fat and lean, beautiful and plain; the brave and the others; those who returned to France because they were too terrified to live here with the Indians, the forest, the dreadful winter; those who have had ten children, or fifteen; those who have lost them all one by one; she who was able to save a single infant out of twelve stillborn—a little girl called Espérance, the name meaning hope, to ward off bad luck, although she died at the age of three months; the one who was shaved and beaten with rods at the town's main crossroads for the crime of adultery; and little Renée Chauvreux, buried in the cemetery on January fifth, 1670, who had come from France on the last ship and was found dead in the snow on the fourth day of January of that same year.

For a long time Flora Fontanges has been convinced that if she could one day gather up all the time that has passed, all of it, rigorously, with all its sharpest details—air, hour, light, temperature, colours, textures, smells, objects, furniture—she should be able to relive the past moment in all its freshness.

Of little Renée Chauvreux, there are very few signs: a mere three lines in the city register and the inventory of her meager trousseau. This *fille du Roi* died in the snow. Her first winter here, her first snow. White beauty that fascinates and kills. Starting with her own childhood in the snow, we should be able to approach Renée Chauvreux, who lies under three feet of powdery snow, if we move stealthily, as lulling and numbing as death itself. But how to awaken the little dead girl lying stiff under ice and time, how make her speak and walk afresh, ask for her secrets of life and death, how tell her she is loved, fiercely, like a child who must be revived?

And thus has Flora Fontanges in the past approached Ophelia, downstream among the drifting flowers, asking the same tormenting question of Ophelia as of Renée Chauvreux, about the bitter destiny of girls. Why?
    One day she took Ophelia into her arms, the arms of a living actress, warmed her with her living breath, made her take back her life and her death, night after night, on a stage that was violently lit for the purpose. Why, in

the case of Renée Chauvreux, can Flora Fontanges not feel all her blood turn to ice in the veins of a little dead girl, surprised by the winter on a sandbar of the Ile d'Orléans, swept by the wind, white as the sky and white as the river and the earth? A single white immensity, as far as the eye can see, in which to lose oneself and die, in a blizzard that erases footsteps one by one.

This time, it is no longer Shakespeare carrying Flora Fontanges. It is a brief statement, as dry as the Civil Code.

Inventory of the goods and possessions of Renée Chauvreux estimated at 250 *livres:*

Two women's costumes, one of Holland stuff, the other of barracan, one shabby skirt of farandine, one very shabby green skirt, one negligée of petersham, one serge camisole, a few linen handkerchiefs, six linen mob-caps and four black coiffes, two of them crepe and two taffeta, a muff of dog fur and two pairs of sheepskin gloves. Did swear in her heart, on her portion of Paradise, that she would not marry Jacques Paviot, soldier in the company of Monsieur de Contrecoeur with whom she has entered into a contract of marriage.

Flora Fontanges carries on her shoulders all the wretchedness of the world, it seems. Why can she not celebrate the joy here, now, in the dying days of summer? Raphaël seems to have recovered from his sorrow over Maud, he dreams of the *filles du Roi,* gazes out at length at the river before him, empty and smooth, where there is no hope of a great sailing ship on the horizon.

"Look how calm the river is, almost like a lake."

It is easy to peer at the river and act as if little Renée Chauvreux were dying inch by inch, like the flame in a votive light that flickers and dies through a coloured glass. This boy shifts from laughter to tears and from tears to laughter with disconcerting ease. Like a child of three.

Raclot, Marie-Madeleine
Turbal, Ursule
Varin, Catherine
Touzé, Jeanne
Raisin, Marguerite

If Flora Fontanges is letting herself be taken over by all these characters again, it is because she needs such mental activity. As long as she is playing a part, her memory will be at rest and her own recollections of joy or sorrow will serve only to nourish lives other than hers. It is quite an accomplishment, being an actress and repressing one's childhood and youth in the city as if they were impure thoughts.

The Lévis hill stands out clear and green against the setting sun. Small pink clouds rush past in the sulphur-coloured sky. The river is marked by the same sulphurous glimmer as the sky, by the same movement of rose-coloured clouds, weightless, with no apparent waves at all.

T<small>HERE'S ROSEMARY, THAT'S FOR RE-</small>
membrance. Pray you, love, remember. And there is pansies, that's for thoughts.

Ophelia appears and disappears, then reappears and disappears once more under Flora Fontanges's closed eyelids, while at her side a boy wearing a blue polo shirt talks on and on about the *filles du Roi.*

Her first role, her first tour. A picture in her mind. A theatre in the provinces in winter, its grey walls covered with saltpetre, where playbills have been posted and a small pocked mirror hung under a frosted bulb. It is freezing in here, as cold as a cave. You can see your breath. How is she to draw Ophelia's gentle face, give her the necessary tear-filled eyes and a mouth gnawed by despair? It is a small mirror crowded with the faces of three actors who are busy painting their faces with all the colours in the rainbow, as if each of them were alone in the world, each with his singular soul, all confused with the powder and greasepaint. It's impossible to put one's makeup on here, with Polonius taking up all the room in the mirror, reeking of garlic and unable to glue on his grey beard, while Hamlet covers his face with diligent sorrow, in a cloud of yellow powder.

Flora Fontanges so much wants Ophelia's passion to be harrowing and true, to be visible on her whole person, clinging to her bones like a second skin. Just next to her, the Queen fails to stuff her opulent bosom inside a close-fitting bodice of threadbare velvet. She swears and spits like an angry cat. Farther away on the stage, behind the closed curtain, you can hear the clatter of weapons, you can hear leaps and muffled cries amid the dust and the veiled illumination from the dimmed stage lights.

These are the good times.

She is twenty-two years old and tonight, after the first performance, she will join a man she loves and who loves her. To play Ophelia she has voluntarily deprived herself of love (imposing her law on the man who is waiting for her) for many days and nights, in the hope that the love and desire in her heart will suffer a thousand deaths, so that she can play Ophelia with all the restrained passion that is necessary. Tonight it is over, Ophelia is offered to the audience in all her touching grace, her utter grief. The curtain is scarcely down, the greasepaint hastily removed, and she has only to throw herself in the arms of this man in trenchcoat and fedora who is waiting impatiently at the stage door. On a small street, rough and ill-paved, in the nearest hotel, a room awaits them, with a high brass bed, a washbasin and bidet, behind a rep curtain flowered in green and red.

"Have there been many men in your life?"

She feels like snapping that she hasn't counted them but that's not true, she has time and again made a precise count, with all the details, odours, sounds, the rooms, sometimes flattened grass, or the back seat of a car. For a long time she thought the cure for love was another love, which is like being healed only to fall sick again. In time, from the farther vantage point of age, it all seems like one single love, quickening repeatedly in its ashes to proclaim either her fever or her boredom.

"What about Maud's father, what was he like?"

Flora Fontanges's voice becomes curt and sharp. She has already got to her feet. Her small head, perched on a long neck, stiffens as if at the end of a staff, and her whole body freezes.

"Like the others, no better or worse. An executive, married, two children, dark-rimmed glasses, heavy beard, olive complexion, cleft chin, vacations, church holidays and weekends with the family, what you'd expect."

What she does not say, what she will not say is that her passion for Maud's father was so violent that during one whole season she played Phaedra with the fury of a devastating flame, being doubly consumed, in her life and in the theatre. Emaciated and burning with fever, she carries her daughter like the fruit of a twofold love, almost dies when the child is born and as soon as she has recovered, takes her to the country, far from the stage and from the father's ungrateful presence.

"I never saw the man again and Maud bears my name."

That is all. She will say no more. Let Raphaël be satisfied with this brief summary of Maud's coming into the world. Let silence settle in like ice forming on the surface of moving water, not only between Raphaël and her but into the very heart of Flora Fontanges, where the slightest stirring of memory could reawaken some rather unattractive scenes between a man and a woman tearing each other to shreds. Each reproaches the other over tiny Maud, who has not yet been born, is the size of a little finger, clinging to her mother's womb like a mussel to its rock. The man would like to make her disappear as if she had never existed, small and insignificant and unseeing as a mollusk. The woman weeps and says over and over that this is her last chance, she will soon be forty and he is a coward. They are most virulent on the subject of precautions, each accusing the other of having acted deliberately. What is between them soon begins to resemble hatred (having built up on both sides, no doubt, for several days), rising to the surface now like an endless garland of green moss that one pulls from the earth. So many recriminations, cries, tears (he accuses her of turning her life into theatre), so many hoarded grudges, so many cutting words, every time.

The era of tumultuous loves is well and truly past. She holds herself erect as if nothing had happened. Wishes with all her might that she could be turned to stone.

Without a single line of her features betraying her, without a flicker of her sea-coloured eyes, safe now from Raphaël's gaze and carefully hidden inside herself, she relives the early days of her motherhood. For three months it was a mad love, and this boy who is Maud's lover cannot have the least idea of such a loving union.

A tiny, isolated house, rented for three months, in the countryside near Tours, hidden in the trees, with a tiny garden of flowers and vegetables. The mother bathes, powders, diapers, rocks, cuddles her daughter, all day long. Talks to her as to a god one adores. Holds her to her naked breast as long as possible, under a loose smock chosen for the purpose. An infinite exchange of warmth and scent. Skin against skin. Gives her the breast with no fixed schedule, like a cat nursing her kitten. Licks her from head to foot. Even claims that if her daughter cries for one moment it is because she has lost track of her mother's odour. For consolation, she takes her tirelessly in her lap as into her natal waters. Will use neither deodorant nor cologne so her daughter can recognize her by her smell alone, animal and warm, hidden away in the countryside, mingled with the perfumes of the earth.

If it is true that most love stories have an end, in this world or the next, the one between Flora Fontanges and her daughter could not last forever. Once they were back in Paris a thousand old demons renewed their attack, just as in the Gospel, and the state of the woman so assailed was worse than before. Contracts argued over and defended. Contracts lost because of maternity leave. Roles to be read and annotated. Fittings. Dinners in town. Solitude interrupted at every turn. A new man looks at her from the corner of a dark green salon. His eyes without colour, merely glittering and mocking, insistent. Nothing is the same now. Time parcelled out. Have them bring my daughter so I may smother her with kisses! The first role after Maud's birth. The pulse that beats in her neck, at the tips of her fingers. No milk. No time. Have them tell the nurse to sterilize the nipples carefully. *The show must go on.* The morning newspaper read at dawn, on a café terrace, with fellow-actors crowding around, eyes blurry with sleep and fatigue. The much-awaited review:

"Madame Fontanges's acting falls short of her abilities, she stands apart from the best that is in her soul, and from her own gestures and her own voice, which is now suddenly reduced to its simplest expression, like a tree stripped of branches. Although she has accustomed us in the past to fully inhabiting her characters, to an excess of light and heat; now her withdrawal, her lack of aura, her awkwardness disappoint us and sadden us. Flora Fontanges's Fantine talks like a ventriloquist, gesticulates like an automaton. Real life is elsewhere."

Her real life is everywhere at once, in the delight at being a mother and the thousand joys and concerns of every day, while yearning for a new man is stirring. She is energetic and vehement, at the heart of her life which is surging from every corner of her being at once. No doubt she is too happy to act another's unhappiness, to weep at the proper moment, and to die under the footlights. She is unable to burst onto the stage with all her blood that is boiling and turning to tears.

Flora Fontanges reads and rereads the review that wounds and offends her. She weeps and clenches her fists. Her fellow actors encourage and console her. She swears she will play Fantine again, this very evening, make the character cry out through her throat and through all the pores of her skin. Even though she is filled with joy because of her little child, just born, she will make the stage resound with the character of Fantine from *Les Misérables*, Fantine, in all her grief, bereft of her daughter and her entire reason for being alive. Flora Fontanges can merely draw from her own childhood, go back where she had promised herself never again to set foot, and Fantine will appear, tonight and tomorrow, facing the audience who will recognize her as she is, filled with tears and sobs.

A tiny article in a morning paper makes her cry out with pleasure.

"Madame Fontanges's Fantine vibrates so powerfully that she takes up our hearts in both hands."

No one will ever know what lost childhood is at stake here or what hidden sorrow has been brought into the light, so carefully and methodically has Flora Fontanges wiped out her traces. Just a portion of unhappiness from the dark night of her memories that is needed to give shape to Fantine and make possible her grim existence. And now the exaltation of acting overwhelms Flora Fontanges with plenitude, as if she were touching the very center of her heart and making it radiate outward upon her face, in her movements, her whole body, like waves unfurling on the sand.

She should have nine lives. Try out each one in turn.
Multiply herself by nine. Nine times nine. Unable to keep
her distance, either from her daughter with her beatific
smile or from Fantine with her heartrending cough. To
dissolve with pleasure as she thinks of the wild and handsome man who sent her a bouquet of huge anemones.
To throw herself in his arms the moment he appears in
the door of her dressing room.

It's an accomplishment to leave Fantine's life and death
behind in the dressing room after the performance, like
cast-off clothing she will pick up tomorrow, at the matinée.
The strange power of metamorphosis. The finest profession
in the world. Flora Fontanges bows to the audience, who
applaud her. The wretched poverty, the miserable tours
have been over for some time now. In an hour she will
be truly in love, still humming with the glamour of the
stage, mad about a man as if it were the first time. And
the desperate lover will think he is touching, on Flora
Fontanges's soft skin, the whole romantic lineage of theatrical and operatic heroines, miraculously delivered into
his arms.

T HE GRANDE-ALLÉE IS LIT UP LIKE a fairground, even though the sun has not completely set over the mountain, behind the parliament buildings. A pink glow trails in the sky and the harsh glare of the street lights cannot drive it away altogether.

Boys and girls cluster on the terraces, while tired horses endlessly drive American tourists about in their calèches.

As they do every evening, Flora Fontanges and Raphaël go from terrace to terrace in the hope of seeing the smooth black head, the small pale face of Maud stand out suddenly, like an apparition, among the young people clustered around their tables.

Someone claims to have seen Maud on Ile aux Coudres, sitting by the road next to the peat marshes. Céleste suggests that Raphaël come to the island with her the next day.

She must face facts, now that the women are no longer there: if the old city and the Grande-Allée have endured with their grey stones and their green shutters, it has been because of the maids. Chambermaids, cooks, nannies, general help, at arms' length they have kept whole streets intact and fresh. There's not an inch of windowpane or mirror, not a single piece of silver or brass they haven't polished and polished again, not a speck of grime or dust that they haven't eradicated and beaten from carpets and furniture, no drape or curtain they haven't washed, blued, starched, and ironed, not a diaper, not a single small flannel blanket they haven't cleaned and bleached. Their main assignment was to make the houses worthy of the most elegant receptions and to make everyday life as exquisite and agreeable as possible. In uniforms of black dresses, white aprons, and caps, they washed, dried, scrubbed, waxed, plucked, boiled and roasted, fried and browned, wiped and rocked, consoled and cared for children and the sick, climbing up and down, day after day, three or four sets of stairs, from cellar to attic.

Now that they have gone, having disappeared little by little over the years, the great, inconvenient houses with all their storeys, impossible to maintain without them, have had to be abandoned.

Some women lost their family names by returning to the city, through the little doorway that led to the Protection of Young Girls. They retained only their Christian names, sometimes changing even these to avoid confusion with the name of Madame or Mademoiselle, in the households which they joined as servants.

Marie-Ange, Alma, Emma, Blanche, Ludivine, Albertine, Prudence, Philomène, Marie-Anne, Clémée, Clophée, Rosana, Alexina, Gemma, Véreine, Simone, Lorina, Julia, Mathilda, Aurore, Pierrette . . .

Ah! how pleasant was the past and how well the Grande-Allée was maintained!

Pierrette Paul escapes her destiny. She will never be a maid in someone's house. Has she not been adopted, according to proper procedures, by M. and Mme Edouard Eventurel?

Raphaël looks at Flora Fontanges's impassive face, her expression suddenly obstinate as she sits there, lost in thought. He is faintly surprised, still under the spell of a litany of women's given names, strange and beautiful, and tries to list them as in a nursery rhyme. Alma, Clémée, Ludivine, Albertine, Aurore . . . He says Aurore and gropes for the next. Repeats Aurore, as if he were expecting someone to appear before him, summoned there by her name.

"Pierrette Paul! You've left out Pierrette Paul!"

She calls it out into the middle of Raphaël's daydream, like someone tossing a pebble into a pond.

"It's a pretty name, Pierrette Paul, don't you think? That was my first role and I've never recovered from it."

She chuckles and drops her head, then looks up at him with a sly, guilty expression. Her voice changes, becomes nasal and drawling, speaking in the country accent.

"Don't give me that look, Raphaël dear. It's just a little girl from the Hospice Saint-Louis, not yet adopted, who's putting in a brief appearance. She's a wretched little creature, quiet as a mouse, an urchin who turns up in my head from time to time and upsets me terribly."

Will she ever accept the entire weight of her life in the dark night of her flesh? Why not evoke instead the Grande-Allée in the time of its splendour, and little Aurore who worked in one of these houses on the other side of the avenue?

They are all clustered there, at the windows and on the steps of the high front stoops. They hold the smallest children in their arms, so they can have a good look. Aurore has barely had time to leave her cardboard suitcase in the room set aside for her in the basement, next to the furnace and the coal chute. She has come to her new situation on the day of a military funeral, and now she is watching and listening, heart pounding and dazed as if she were about to fall. Even at her village church she has never seen or heard the like. As if the sky were about to be torn open. The usual mass of grey or blue is split from top to bottom, as if to make room for the northern lights. The other side of the world shows itself and is heard, with its heartrending music, its solemn procession. Most poignant, unquestionably, are the sword and cap laid across a gun carriage, covered with a white cloth on which are drawn stripes and crosses of red and blue which little Aurore does not yet know to be a foreign flag. Slowly the procession is making its way towards the hereafter, she thinks, and the military music plays on and on, wrenching our hearts.

Aurore blows her nose and wipes her eyes, her bosom rises and falls inside her black sateen bodice. The son of the household looks at her, half smiling under his blonde mustache.

This girl is doing it deliberately too. How is it possible to be at once so slender and so round? Each of her movements traces marvels in the air with just enough energy and softness to bewitch us. The son of the household, a law student, follows her from room to room the minute he has the chance! How is it possible, in his father's house, to allow an unknown creature of seventeen to move about so freely before us? She stretches her arm to draw the curtain in the sitting room and you can see the outline of her breast as it moves under the bib of her embroidered apron; she kneels to dust the coffee table and the line of her back describes a perfect arc. But when she hunkers down to wash the kitchen linoleum and her little behind is higher than her head, he thinks such ease of movement should only be possible during a night of love, and then not in a respectable bed, while the smell of sweat that accompanies even the slightest movement of a lusty partner transports us out of this world.

But the moment when it becomes utterly unbearable is one Saturday morning, on the main staircase that goes from the ground floor. The highly polished banister gleams dully, the green carpet, freshly swept with tea leaves, stretches tightly from step to step, held in place by strips of shiny brass. She is there, halfway up the staircase, holding a rag and the brass polish. She is rubbing and humming, her lips closed. She does not hear him. He was just passing by as he went to fetch a book, and here she is barring his way. A warmth behind her draws nearer, a warm breathless mass is draped over her shoulders, her back, her loins. She stifles a cry. Straightens. Turns. Flattens her back against the dark panelling of the staircase. The boy's pale face is there, very close, scalded looking, as if he has just shaved. He seizes her wrists. He breathes in her odour and it is everything he loves. He murmurs Aurore, as if he has lost his voice. It is at this moment that Madame comes down, rustling her skirts. Aurore disappeared at once with her rag and her flask. He has only enough time to spy in passing a restless little sunbeam that darts here and there over the staircase, dancing from the brass strips to the reflected shimmer and the copper glow of Aurore's chestnut hair.

And I rub you and I polish you and finally I touch you, not with a rag now but with my two bare hands, and all your skin from top to toe, gleams like brass, like gold, like the sun and the moon, it shivers with russet light and it is so good we could die of pleasure. He can still dream. He's a young man of good standing who studies the law in his closed room. He is blind before his open book, so obsessed, so haunted is he by Aurore. The Civil Code prevents nothing. It is useless to study the law when one already lives outside the law, in the violent regions of the self where desire is the only master.

He will fail his year-end examination.

All that Flora Fontanges says and does since she first met Raphaël is an attempt to appropriate the city along with him. They have summoned creatures now disappeared, drawing them out by their names, as with a rope from the bottom of a well, to bring them on stage, bowing and speaking their names aloud so they may be recognized and acknowledged before disappearing again. In this way do obscure heroines of history come to life and then die, one by one. Now it is the turn of little Aurore to gesture to us from the depths of her violent death.

This time it is not the history student who evokes the past, but Flora Fontanges, whose memory is unreliable and concerns her selectively, depending on whether or not the fear of compromising herself forces her to ransack the memories of others, helter skelter, along with her own, until all memories grow unrecognizable.

Selective from memory

"My false grandmother used to tell stories in my presence as if she were talking to the wall through me, as if I were transparent, but she told them so well, with so much pent-up passion."

"And little Aurore?"

Little Aurore suddenly shifts to the middle ground in the heart of Flora Fontanges, as a tall old woman, very erect, bony and white, rises and begins to speak. Little Aurore's tragic end seems to have been evoked by a strange voice as Flora Fontanges drones on, word after word, as if she were listening to each one being dictated in turn from the shadows of her memory.

"On the day she turned eighteen little Aurore's body was found, raped and murdered, in Victoria Park, near the St. Charles River. Police investigations were fruitless. The murderer was never apprehended. The case of Aurore Michaud, daughter of Xavier and Maria Michaud, who was born at Sainte-Croix-de-Lotbinière on August seventh, 1897, and died on September seventh, 1915, was quickly closed."

The news caused horrified shudders, from the upper town to the lower town, providing fuel for conversation for days and days. But ordinary life, after being briefly withdrawn, reclaimed its rights, like water after a pebble falls.

People are cared for with mustard plasters, with leeches, with flax seeds, syrup of creosote, and balsam of tolu, women give birth at home and remain two weeks in bed after the confinement, girls study the piano (for boys, it's not worth the trouble, it makes them effeminate), funerals, weddings, and christenings are numerous, life and death jostle one another in the porticoes along the Grande-Allée and in the old city, the most stable fortunes are bound up with income from the land, down below, in the seigneuries. The elder Madame Eventurel promised her only daughter, Elodie, that she could have a blue silk gown as soon as the notary had given her the year's rent from the farmers.

WHAT SORT OF DREAM IS IT, TO act as if one had never been alive in the city, to create a vacuum? thinks Flora Fontanges, who has just brought to life a clear, sharp image of the elder Madame Eventurel. Perhaps she need only concentrate on the Grande-Allée as it is today, in the company of Raphaël and Céleste, and she will escape from the house on the Esplanade. Will no angel ever utter in her ear the remark, blessed above all others: "The past no longer exists"? How can she not imagine, occasionally, the leap of joy of the prisoner who breaks her chains, becomes free and light, without memory, aware only of the night falling over the city?

Raphaël has walked away with Céleste. They are making plans to go together to Ile aux Coudres. She sits by herself, at a table on the café terrace. She feels intensely alone. The moment no longer supports her. From here she has no choice but to return in spirit to the house on the Esplanade, as if it were no longer in her power not to go there, summoned by her indestructible, stubborn childhood.

A little girl sits on a stool at the feet of an old woman, in the chalky silence of the house on the Esplanade. The steady rhythm of a great ebony clock. The vacant air of Sunday enters everywhere, slips under doors, through the cracks of windows, it throbs, massive and hollow in chimneys.

She is a little girl who escaped from the fire at the Hospice Saint-Louis in 1927.

She has been without roots forever and she dreams of a great tree anchored in the night of the earth, beneath the city, lifting the asphalt from sidewalks and streets with only the dark wisp of its subterranean breath. This tree with its gnarled trunk would stand higher than the towers of the parliament buildings, dense with branches, boughs and twigs, with leaves and wind. Perhaps the little girl might even be the single bird at the top of this tree, rustling with breezes, for already she desires more than anything to sing and tell the story of the life that is in the tree, making it her very own, her family tree and personal history.

This sometimes happens on Sunday afternoon, in the house on the Esplanade. The adoptive parents are at vespers or visiting, depending on the day, and the false grandmother is tending the little girl. The false grandmother describes so well the bright and shady sides of the Eventurel family, evoking her own childhood and youth and those of her father and mother, as far back as the first days of the colony, declaring that in the seventeenth century the seigneury at Beauport already belonged to her own blood, planted in the earth like a tree in May. The little girl, without father or mother, who sits at the old lady's feet, longs to appropriate the Eventurels' tree for herself, the way one takes possession of one's own property when it has been seized by thieves, in dark times of severe injustice.

Soon, from Sunday to Sunday, the old lady's stories extended to the whole city, as she took pleasure in recalling *habitant* life in all its ramifications. The little girl's ambition grew with the growing fullness of the stories. Soon she dreamed the extravagant dream of having her imaginary possessions extend to an entire society, the way one turns over family matters, births, marriages, and deaths, she herself concerned from generation to generation, building a past for herself that consists of several generations and of solid alliances with the whole city.

But the little girl fell from her perch when the lady from the Esplanade dropped her impassioned and engaging storyteller's voice in favour of her everyday metallic tone to tell M. and Mme Eventurel, home from their Sunday calls:

"The child never opens her mouth; it's a waste to give her lessons in diction and music, she'll never learn how to speak and sing as you'd like, nor even to listen politely. Whenever I say a word she seems to throw herself at it, as if it were a bone to be gnawed. Oh yes, that hunger of hers is very shocking, like a stray dog's. And as I've told you before, you'll never make a lady of her."

One day the little girl was witness to the old lady's solitude. The door that opened onto the upstairs hallway was ajar, revealing part of the mysterious place to which Madame Eventurel liked to retire. From the door one could see very clearly the old rose boudoir, barely lit. Muted glimmers seeped onto the flowered carpet. A great black clock with hands, numbers, and pendulum of gleaming brass stood against a bare wall. Madame Eventurel was sitting there, facing the clock, very straight in an old rose-velvet wing chair. She was listening to the time that passes and never returns. Madame Eventurel's attention to the tick-tock of the clock was total and obsessive, as if she were following the beating of her own endangered heart in her old woman's breast. A sort of solemn ceremony between Madame Eventurel and her ebony clock. The fear of being hurled into death from one moment to the next if a single tick-tock of the great clock were skipped. She was watching her death approach <u>her as in a mirror</u>, she was listening to her pulse outside of her, as if it appeared on a screen. It was her wish to look her death in the eye, and she dreaded the shock of its coming.

The little girl was convinced she had just unearthed a dreadful secret. When on Sunday she found herself alone with her false grandmother, she feared the revelation of that secret, concealed perhaps in one of the old lady's stories.

Sometimes the old lady would interrupt herself abruptly, marking a long peevish silence before she picked up the thread of her story. As the silence persisted, the little girl thought she could hear Madame Eventurel concentrating hard on spiteful remarks about her.

In reality Madame Eventurel was musing that the little girl sitting on a stool at her feet should never have been born, that it was inconceivable for her to try to ingrain herself into one of the oldest families in the city.

Although Madame Eventurel never addressed the little girl, she would sometimes talk about her in her presence, calling her "the little schemer."

IT'S NOT THAT SHE IS ILL, BUT since Raphaël and Céleste left for Ile aux Coudres, she has shut herself away in her hotel room and refused to emerge.

In the solitude and the night of rue Sainte-Anne broad sweeps of memory give way as she lies in the dark, surrendered, bound hand and foot to old images that assail her.

The dead women make a noise in her throat. She names them one by one, and the companions of her childhood come as their names are called, from tall to short, intact and untouched by fire, wearing the same black serge uniform, white collars and cuffs, black ribbed stockings and laced boots, their short hair carefully bobbed every month.

Alfreda Thibault
Laurette Levasseur
Jacqueline Racine
Marie-Marthe Morency
Théodora Albert
Jeanne-d'Arc Racine
Estelle Roy
Corinne Picard
Georgette Auclair
Germaine Létourneau
Marie-Jeanne Binet . . .

All must be named aloud, and a witness must be present to hear them, the names of these children who were burned alive, and we must gather them to our hearts.

Raphaël is no longer there to share her evocation of the little girls from the Hospice Saint-Louis. Now that it's a question of her own life, she is alone, with neither pity nor compassion.

A long string of little girls dressed in mourning surround Flora Fontanges's bed on rue Sainte-Anne. The tallest, though, wears a blue smock cinched at the waist by a belt and she has curly hair. Her name is Rosa Gaudrault and she will be burned along with the children from the lower forms. She says "kitten, sweetheart, pet, my treasure, my lovely, my angel," she laughs and talks very softly because the orphanage rules forbid giving the children any names but the ones inscribed in the register. At times she sings "the Blessed Virgin soon will come, with her long hair hanging down" and she is radiant as a bluebird in a black flock of starlings.

"Rosa," says Flora Fontanges, holding out her arms in the night, and she weeps.

Who would venture across the live coals except Rosa Gaudrault, who has already made the gift of her life and renews it continually?

She is sixteen years old. She goes in and out, bringing children every time, passes through the flames and smoke, a wet cloth over her face. She calls them by name, begs them to come with her, she who is kind and good and has always thought of them as normal children with father and mother at their side and a normal house filled with laughter and warmth. She calls to them. Takes them in her arms. Pulls them outside. Goes back inside with a wet cloth that freezes along the way. She is calling still. Begging them to come outside with her. Even the firemen with their masks and long ladders do not have her courage and her daring.

When they found Rosa Gaudrault the next day in the

rubble, there were two little girls in her arms who had burned to death with her, covered with ice, a single branch, gnarled and black.

"Dead wood! There, there!"

Fever overcomes her and makes her rave. She is writhing in the brand-new white bed with brass knobs at its corners. She is eleven years old. M. and Mme Edouard Eventurel have just adopted her and bought her a bed. She is a little girl who was rescued from the fire in the Hospice Saint-Louis.

"If the fever doesn't drop I guarantee nothing," says the doctor.

There remains just a slim margin of life wherein she struggles, tormented by invisible flames that burn her and consume her. She begins to cry out again in a voice that is harrowing, insistent, that is not of this world. She begs them to take away the unbearable thing from the foot of her bed. She holds out her arm towards the chair on which her new clothes lie folded, cries out in a voice from beyond the grave:

"There, there! Dead wood!"

"If death should occur, wrap the body in a sheet soaked in carbolic acid."

They will do what must be done. In the event of life or death. Have they not adopted her according to proper procedure, so that she will bear their name and become their daughter, with full rights? A nurse watches over her, day and night. In the next room M. and Mme Eventurel wait for word, hour by hour. Now and then they lift a corner of the sheet, soaked in disinfectant, that hangs in the doorway and isolates the sick child's room from the rest of the apartment. They look at her for a moment, sitting up in bed, her arm stretched out towards the chair on which her clothes are laid.

"Dead wood, there!"

"Rosa," the little girl will say again, over and over, in the bedroom with flowered wallpaper made ready for her by M. and Mme Eventurel.

Then, nothing.

Nothing more at all. As the fever drops and her skin peels away in strips. Not another word. As if she had become mute following the scarlet fever. As if she had forgotten everything of her past. As if the present were a *glaring and empty place* wherein one need only be silent.

No sounds seem able now to escape from her throat, as she tears long strands of dead skin from her hands and feet. Must she not slough the skin of her whole body and even renew the inside of her body where her small past life lies hidden? When she has been turned inside out and made new, perhaps she will be able to exist a second time and say: "Here, here I am, this is me. I am alive again, pulled from the dead, snatched from the flames." Is this the way M. and Mme Eventurel want her to be, subject to no ancient law, fresh as a newborn, without past or memory, as easy to read as an open book, reborn through their good will, planted firmly upon a known road that was chosen in advance and marked out by them?

They have taken every precaution that she will never be the same. A full quarantine, eight days longer than the doctor's prescription. Forty-eight days exactly, shut away in a bedroom, with a new doll and a magazine to read. Delirium and fever have erased all the horror and fear. This child needs only them to begin life anew. They have only to bring her naked from her bedroom, after they have shaved her hair.

They call her Marie Eventurel, speaking under their breath, not yet daring to name her aloud for fear of startling her. Both are waiting for her to come out of quarantine. A long time ago the notice "Scarlet Fever" was posted on the apartment on rue Bourlamaque, a long time ago she came to them reclusive and delirious and now she emerges from her room, bringing nothing, as they have instructed her. Her true life is beginning at this very moment and everything that has happened before today must disappear along with the mattress, the sheets and blankets, the nightgown and the doll, taken away by the city's sanitation department which will carry out the disinfection.

Her black hair, newly shorn, strews the floor of the bedroom, her nightgown forms a circle on the ground about her feet. For the first time since her birth she is naked from head to foot. She is ashamed and dares not move. Now she is being called to come out of the quarantine room. She does not yet have her own name, she is between two names, the old one having been consigned with the objects to be destroyed, the new one not yet ready to be assumed. They summon her, but not by name, and she must take a step, then two, stride over her nightgown on the floor. She is eleven years old. During her illness she became terribly thin. Her pelvic bones jut out under her white skin. They call her. Tell her to come. Her shaven skull is like ivory.

She must walk along the corridor. Each step is torture and she suffers from her nakedness as if she has been flayed alive, summoned to appear before strangers nude, defenceless, stripped to the bone, it seems to her. She walks toward the bathroom which smells of javel water. The nurse immerses her and washes her, scouring her generously with sulphured soap. Disinfected now from head to foot, she still carries the smell of chlorine on her skin and on the fresh linen and the new dress in which she has just been clad.

And now M. and Mme Eventurel advance, the two of them together, to kiss her and bid her welcome. They discover a child of silence and ice, petrified.

THE NIGHT WAS VILE IN THE HOTEL on rue Sainte-Anne, thronged with nightmares and apparitions. Now the day is coming; its sound, its odour rap at the door and the closed window. The din of a vacuum cleaner and of keys clattering in the hallway, the hum of cars, blurred voices from the street. Her legs, her arms are heavy under the sheets, as if poorly drawn, formless. Dry-mouthed. A new day is breaking. She turns to face the wall. Enjoys the deep darkness. Refuses to get up.

She will spend three days in bed in her hotel room, while chambermaids grow impatient and tirelessly knock at the door.

"Can I make up the room?"

Until now, there was no real danger in bringing the women of the city to life as defenceless creatures mingled with her own flesh, to make them sing with us. Even though there was just one spectator facing her, it had taken place on stage. Raphaël was going along with the game like the archangel he is, with his dazzling smile and his great invisible folded wings.

Now that she has nothing more to invent, she is alone in the dark closed room. The imaginary women of the city escape her and dissolve into crumbs.

She clings to the night as to a dwelling place. The blackness of the night surrounds her, moves over her face, her body, sticky and opaque, it enters her veins, turns to shadows the vermilion root of her heart. Flora Fontanges is haunted, becomes herself the dead of the night, open and welcoming.

Above all, do not let the daylight in. Come to terms with the night, once and for all. Now that she is alone in the city. Flush out all the ghosts. Become brand-new and fresh again on the land that gave her birth, as on the first day, without memory.

The story to come has no visible thread, is apparently unravelled, gleaming and quick, like mercury which breaks apart, re-forms and flees.

THE IDEA OF ADOPTING AN OR-
phan girl occurred to them on the night of the fire, when
the Hospice Saint-Louis was burning and it was impossible
to get out all the little girls who were imprisoned by the
flames. Those who could be saved were wrapped at once
in blankets, coats, men's jackets, whatever could be found,
and dispersed to hospitals, convents, hotels, families.

Dr. Simard brought home three little girls. The
Eventurels, who were visiting the doctor that evening, were
able to choose among the three at leisure.

The oldest had no more tears. She stared straight ahead,
her eyes as dull as a statue's. Her lips were as white as
her cheeks. Draped in a rug that she refused to shed,
shuddering violently as if someone were shaking her from
head to foot, she displayed the utmost dignity. Head erect,
hands crossed on her breast, wordless, motionless, neither
eating nor drinking nor replying when spoken to, she was
there because that was where she had been placed, and
she must be there because there was no longer any other
place in the world for her to live and die. If weariness
sometimes caused her head to droop she would straighten
it at once, and that abrupt move gave her a certain haugh-
tiness that pleased the Eventurels.

Madame Eventurel talked about innate distinction and Dr. Simard alluded to the formidable pride of some of the poor, to whom one cannot offer charity.

No one consulted her. She was transplanted from the Hospice Saint-Louis to the Eventurels' small apartment on rue Bourlamaque. The authorities concerned agreed to the transfer and the adoption. She was struck down by scarlet fever almost immediately. Delirium allowed her to cry out her pain and her dread. As the fever dropped, silence took hold of her again and did not leave for days and days. The time it took for her hair to grow back, the time it took to learn the Eventurels' language and manners.

Without ever uttering a word, she crossed out in her head all the ones that occurred to her, on this or that occasion when M. and Mme Eventurel used other words that she didn't know but retained as soon as she'd heard them, as if she were learning a foreign language.

One does not say: "I ain't, supper, her and me, sweat, I should of went." Rather one says: "I'm not, dinner, she and I, perspire, I should have gone." One does not dream of an American Beauty satin dress which would be vulgar, instead one selects a kilt from Holt Renfrew made of genuine Scottish tartan. Indeed, whatever is Scottish or English is entirely acceptable. As for the Irish, that's another kettle of fish. One does not eat with one's knife. One does not swing one's shoulders when walking. One does not crack one's knuckles. One removes one's nightgown before taking a bath. One does not prefer potatoes, molasses, and porridge to any unfamiliar dish that appears on the table.

One Sunday at the dining-room table, in the middle of the meal, all at once she broke the silence. She asked in a clear voice:

"May I please have a little *charlotte russe?*"

It sounded as fine to her as her first lines on stage. She who had never seen either theatre or cinema suddenly found herself able to play the part the Eventurels intended for her. She was now becoming their daughter, with full rights, after waiting in silence for perfect mastery of their speech so she could talk to them as an equal, a child from the same world or so she thought, and nothing would show her up or incriminate her.

The first day at school, when she was asked her name, she replied in an exceedingly clear, loud voice:

"My name is Marie Eventurel."

It started with a name that was given to her and that she took, and little by little she began to resemble Marie Eventurel, as people wished her to.

At prize-giving her new name, Marie Eventurel, was heard often, called out from the stage because she won almost all the prizes, even the first prize for piano and music. Singing, in particular, filled her with delight. It seemed to her that if she worked hard, one day she would be free to do anything with her voice, vocal flourishes and trills allowing her to express her whole life and the whole world, unfurled in its terrible magnificence through her throat.

When it was time to recite a poem in class or to explain a text, she came to adore the sounds and the words that formed in her mouth, on her tongue and teeth. She sometimes felt she had a vocation to speak and to sing, and there was nothing on earth more beautiful than human speech, full and resonant. She sang hymns one moment and love songs the next, like a saint in heaven or a romantic lover. She closed her eyes and her face was radiant. For a few moments, she possessed the earth.

At the Eventurels' house, what was done at the orphanage must be undone, she must conduct herself as if she had never before known how to live and was just beginning to breathe. They sometimes said, quite frankly, that she was on the other side of the earth. The wrong side of the world, that must be it; the reverse of everything she has been required to learn up till now.

Madame Eventurel said:

"Don't shut your eyes when someone speaks to you."

Useless to plead that at the orphanage they had to keep their gaze lowered as much as possible, above all never look one's superiors in the eye. At the Eventurels', the same law does not prevail, never again will the same law prevail, anywhere in the world. Draw a line through it once and for all. Look instead at the lovely things around her, books, dolls, games, roller skates and ice skates, and such pretty white paper with pink flowers and blue birds on her bedroom walls.

When her hair had grown long enough, curling over her forehead and ears, she was taken for the first time to Madame Eventurel's mother, in the house on the Esplanade. She stood for a long moment, very straight, facing the old lady who seemed to look through the little girl and see something troubling on the wall behind the child.

At table, even as she was sampling dishes she found distasteful, she felt very strongly that she no longer existed at all, neither as Pierrette Paul nor as Marie Eventurel, but was becoming a sort of transparent shadow sitting opposite an old woman who looked like the Queen of Hearts in *Alice in Wonderland*.

Everyone who lived in the city filed through the grownups' conversation in the proper order. Some of the individuals who were conjured up had to undergo a severe examination by the old lady on the Esplanade, before the pitiless verdict.

"Not distinguished!" she declared in a peremptory tone.

The little girl thought she was hearing the Queen of

Hearts pronounce the death sentence:

"Off with their heads!"

She must have heard that sentence directed at her on the day in question, as they were leaving the house on the Esplanade. Just as Madame Eventurel was sticking a long pin into her hat and adjusting the veil over her face, the old lady came up to her daughter, pretending to whisper, but the acid voice seeped out on all sides and in all directions:

"You'll never make a lady of her."

She knew the Queen of Hearts was condemning her to have her head cut off.

Alice lost in wonderland

T HEY PROMISED THEMSELVES THAT they would do their duty, despite all opposition, and take their adopted daughter to her debut and her marriage. They had set their minds to it quite firmly.

"We'll make a real little lady of her," declares Monsieur Eventurel, who enjoys repeating the English words used by his mother-in-law.

Twenty times a day, Marie Eventurel wonders if she walks properly like a lady, if she bows properly like a lady, if she smiles properly like a lady, if she eats properly like a lady. It's exhausting, like being a painter's model asked to hold a pose for long hours.

In another life she had got used to watching how she moved and spoke, watching even her most secret thoughts, in the hope of becoming like those saints, ecstatic and radiant despite the seven blades that pierce them. That was at the Hospice Saint-Louis, and Mother Marie-des-Neiges was reading the lives of the saints from the rostrum in the refectory at meal time. She felt the same tension in her whole being, the same dizzying yearning to leave her self behind and burst into the light, the same thrusting towards the divine absolute, the same weariness immediately after the searing flash, when harsh reality extended all around the child born at the Miséricorde.

The bare walls of the refectory, the great black cross above the rostrum, the endless tables, the wooden benches on which were crowded a hundred little girls in black, hunched over the sour cabbage soup and the grey meat. Pierrette Paul was sure she would never be summoned into the parlour on Sunday, not in this life or the next one either, she would add on nights of despair.

There was only Rosa Gaudrault who consoled her and called her, in secret, my kitten and my treasure.

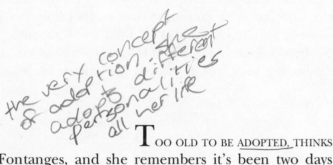
the very concept of adoption that adopts different personalities all her life

Too OLD TO BE ADOPTED, THINKS Flora Fontanges, and she remembers it's been two days since Raphaël has come to ask about her.

She turns to face the wall. Shuts her eyes. Picks up the thread of her story. In the dark, sees again the Eventurels who pretend they have a daughter of their own.

Too old to love and to be loved.

They should have taken a newborn. She is more than eleven years old. Too late. For her and for them. A certain distance that must be crossed, on both sides. That will never be crossed. Accept the inevitable. Beneath the implacable eye of the old lady on the Esplanade.

Lying in their big brass bed, under the pink eiderdown swollen with choice feathers, M. and Mme Eventurel frequently, at night, examine their conscience. They ask themselves if they have done all that is necessary to make their adopted daughter sweet and pliable, worthy of her appointed place in society.

While Marie Eventurel sleeps in the little room with its walls covered in flowers and birds, she utters occasional cries she does not remember on awakening.

"I must have dreamed about the wolf," she says in the

morning, shrugging, when when last night's bad dreams
are recalled.

In reality it is little girls who pass through her dreams,
who are set alight like torches. Seven are chosen to play
the part of the seven tongues of fire of Pentecost. It is a
classroom session organized by Mother Marie-des-Neiges.
Their hair blazes like straw. Their nightgowns drift away
like burned paper. The smell of their scorched flesh fills
all the space. Someone says that the greatest gift of Pentecost
is wisdom, which contains all other gifts in one bright
flame.

Marie Eventurel screams in her sleep.   *Mary*

During the day she is as wise and well-behaved as if she
were filled with the seven gifts of the Holy Ghost. There
is no doubt about her wisdom or her good behaviour.
Whenever she sings in school or in church, whenever she
recites a poem in class, an alchemy occurs in her, stirring
together tears and cries to produce a true, crystalline voice
that is bewitched by its own pleasing tone and by the fact
that her soul is escaping into the light of day in a pure
breath.

*all this St. imiginary goes
with her name St. Mary.*

*— The st. is an actor, set on
a stage to be played or burned.*

Breakfast has been brought to her. She half-opens the window. Looks out blindly onto the street. Sets the breakfast tray on her knees. Sits up against the open window. She sees nothing of what is going on in the street. Eats her food without tasting it. Is quite unaware of what is in the room. Fully engaged in telling herself the story of M. and Mme Eventurel.

I know a few things about them, she thinks, and feels an urge to laugh.

First of all, it is important to note that the only daughter of the old lady on the Esplanade married her first cousin, to salvage the Eventurel name which was disappearing.

Flora Fontanges is utterly aloof. As if little characters made of wood have come to visit her in her hotel room and are moving before her now like puppets.

Monsieur Eventurel sometimes leaves the house very early in the morning, standing by the kitchen sink to gulp his coffee. Since the maid's departure, Monsieur Eventurel has stopped eating breakfast. Madame Eventurel takes too long to prepare the meal. Monsieur Eventurel doesn't have time to wait. No more orange juice, velvety porridge, fragrant toast. Monsieur Eventurel is as anxious to leave the apartment on rue Bourlamaque as if he were going to punch in at a factory. Often, he regrets that he once told Madame Eventurel she has the bearing of a queen. Since then, she has never walked quickly.

Monsieur Eventurel knows the city inside out, in all its twists and turns, ascending and descending from the upper town to the town below and from the lower town to the upper town, listening, questioning anyone, everyone he encounters, from nine in the morning until five at night.

It often started with a funeral that Monsieur Eventurel would follow, walking bareheaded, summer or winter. The life of the dead man was immediately commented upon and dissected sotto voce, his family tree assembled and disassembled, in order and disorder, along with former classmates encountered in the procession or at the church. It's amazing how, some days—assuming you have the time— by following a hearse, you can find yourself providing an almost flawless account of the past events in the life of one of the city's dead, sometimes blithely going back several generations.

Once the dead man has come to his final resting place, Monsieur Eventurel and a few friends might end up in the bar of the Château or the Clarendon. News items and the politics of the land were subjects of lively discussion. Over a cup of coffee or a glass of gin.

The waiter sometimes joined in, and he was listened to religiously. He would lean across the bar, bring his bright red face as close as possible, drop his voice, and shamelessly expose the city's secret lives, the ones kept jealously tucked away, but which slip out one night when you're drunk and feeling low, amid cigarette smoke, the smell of beer.

"In here, nothing gets lost."

And the waiter touches his forehead in a broad and solemn gesture.

The sources of Monsieur Eventurel's information proved to be many and surprising. Bankers, lawyers, brokers, exchange officers were heard and consulted on every detail of Monsieur Eventurel's business. He closely followed prices on the Stock Exchange and invested and transferred his fortune with no rhyme or reason. It sometimes took him all day. From time to time he was distracted by intrigues he discovered here and there, through business conversations, lunches at the University Club or private chats with secretaries and elevator boys, to whom he was always considerate.

Some days, after a particularly solemn funeral, a very sad Monsieur Eventurel, realizing suddenly that you can't take your money to heaven, would decide to ignore business matters for the rest of the day and let the thread of time unfurl according to the inspiration of the moment.

Sometimes he would search for a perfect rose, going from florist to florist along the city streets. This quest for the absolute could take him the whole morning. Around noon, tired and drunk with perfume, fingers pricked by thorns, he would resign himself to selecting the heaviest, most fragrant rose that he could find, one he could offer with his best wishes to some old lady from an excellent background who lived in seclusion now, in the General Hospital. Once the rose had been offered and received with the appropriate emotion and gratitude, Monsieur Eventurel would turn the moment to his advantage and garner the old lady's confidences. That was how he learned that the notary was at this very moment at the bedside of poor Alice D. who wasn't long for this world. But what most stirred the heart of Monsieur Eventurel was being informed in the old lady's whispering voice of the fate that lay in store for poor Alice D.'s eldest son, who had been cut off by his mother. The old lady's voice almost vanished and she'd swear

she'd heard it all through the door of the room next to
hers.

"As for you, Charles my son, you've already cost me
plenty, I'm disinheriting you."

After he left the General Hospital, Monsieur Eventurel
would take the streetcar to the Petit Champlain, where
he would find Gladys, his parents' former maid, who raised
hens and rabbits in her kitchen and never left her wheel-
chair. Gladys was a veritable mine of gossip and intrigue,
fed on it, every morning, by her taxi-driver husband who
worked nights.

Stirred by Gladys's chatter, half-English, half-French,
often trivial and crude, Monsieur Eventurel would decide
to round off the afternoon at Georgiana's on rue Saint-Paul,
in what Madame Eventurel would call a bad house.

Without dropping one centimetre of his great height,
hat in hand, his expression at once contrite and nervous,
buttoned into his steel grey, white-striped jacket, Monsieur
Eventurel would make his entrance. He was greeted at
Georgiana's threshold by exclamations of delight. He was
called "My Lord" and "Your Majesty," which pleased him
enormously.

Madame Eventurel never suspected a thing, convinced
that what went on between Monsieur Eventurel and the
girls of rue Saint-Paul could only take place at night, in
shuttered houses where red lights drew the attention of
bad boys.

Madame Eventurel's husband came home every evening
around six, weighed down by the burdens of the day like
any punctual, diligent worker.

Evenings at the Eventurels' were most lively. The couple
greedily exchanged news. Madame Eventurel was rich with
all the telephone calls she had made in the course of the
day.

When the Eventurels were once again recumbent statues

beneath the pink eiderdown, they experienced an extreme satisfaction, an infinite security, so evident and firmly sewn were the numerous threads that attached them to the city. They seemed unaware that there were other places on the planet Earth on which to set one's feet by day and close one's eyes by night.

On long winter evenings, in the stale air of the small blue-papered Victorian salon, the remarks exchanged by M. and Mme Eventurel would sometimes drift and hum like drowsy flies. In the next room, huddled over her books and scribblers, their adopted daughter seemed to want to know nothing about the city's stories. She cared about only one secret, the secret of her birth, and that would never be revealed to her or to the Eventurels, despite their research.

All that they know, all they will ever know, is that the child born at the Miséricorde was later taken in by nuns already burdened with all the sins of the world, dedicated to the expiation and the salvation of all, placed on the cross every day with Our Lord. And innocent and tender little children were borne by them, bodily, like surplus crosses.

The Eventurel couple never lost sight of the line that demarcates good society from ordinary people and from those who were, quite bluntly, common. Clearly stratified in this way, the city remained reassuring and clear in the hearts of the Eventurels, as if the order of the world were rooted there.

M. and Mme Eventurel fell asleep, perfectly calm and serene as in the waters that gave them birth.

ONE DAY, THOUGH, THE ORDER
of the world was almost overthrown, and Monsieur
Eventurel came close to being swept away by the upheaval,
driven to the brink of ruin and tossed in with people who
had next to nothing.

"Money's not producing any more," he would repeat,
astonished.

A series of bad investments over the years had pitted
Monsieur Eventurel against the depression that was rav-
aging the country, and the image of his fall from grace
rose before Monsieur Eventurel all day long and even at
night, while he slept.

They had to leave rue Bourlamaque and move to rue
Plessis, to a smaller apartment.

Madame Eventurel takes bitter pleasure in calling to
mind the stages in her decline from rue des Remparts,
which she had to abandon, sick at heart, two years after
her marriage, because of her husband's financial negligence. And now what she fears most of all is to be driven
from the upper town one day by a fiery angel yielding a
sword, and never be able to return, to her ruin and despair.

From now on, in evening conversations between the
Eventurels, the phrases "come down in the world" and

"cleaned out" occur often, flung violently into the man's face by his wife. And the little girl doing her homework in the dining room next door thinks these unfamiliar words are horrible insults or curses.

In his present humiliated state, Monsieur Eventurel would give his soul to be called "My Lord" or "Your Majesty" again. But Monsieur Eventurel can't afford now to go to Georgiana, on rue Saint-Paul.

If Marie Eventurel is growing in wisdom, fierce wisdom that makes her silent, studious and obstinate, her movements are graceless and hobbled. Gone now for reasons of economy are the too-costly lessons in singing and diction, gone are the moments of freedom when she would escape from herself to become in turn Angélique, Ophelia, Catarina, Beline, Rosette, Armande, or Henriette. With no room of her own now, sleeping in the dining room, with no place to escape to in the tiny apartment on rue Plessis, Marie Eventurel lives her adolescence as if she were disappearing into the night. Her cramped movements are those of a prisoner under constant surveillance. Only much later, when she has become Flora Fontanges, across the sea, will her body be restored to her in all its lightness.

It is the sea water, that allows her to escape the city

And here she is now, old. Back at home in the city that gave her birth. The circle is complete. Her final role is before her, to be learned and allowed to infuse like the bitter tea-leaves at the bottom of a cup, for telling fortunes. She leafs through the slim volume of *Happy Days*. She knows what is in store. She is Winnie, deep inside herself. She is afraid. She collects her thoughts before climbing onto her sand pile and burying herself, grain by grain.

Her face in the bathroom mirror over the basin advances towards her, as if through a window; it is an image detached from herself, to be seen and recognized by her. Well aware that time is short. Such great weariness on her features. She turns her head. Picks up *Happy Days*. Becomes exercised at the futility of everything, long after she has closed the book. — *Beckett*

The sounds and smells of the city drift in through the wide-open window.

H E SAYS: "I'VE COME TO SEE HOW you are. We're just back from the Ile d'Orléans and we're leaving again right away. Céleste is downstairs."

He stands in the doorway holding a small bouquet of wildflowers.

She is wearing a terrycloth robe. Her eyes are puffy. Her short hair stands up in tufts on her head.

She asks in a thin voice that seems not to belong to her:

"And Maud?"

"She was already gone when we got there. She can't be far away. We'll find her. We'll cover Charlevoix County village by village. Céleste and I thought some flowers . . ."

She says:

"Look, don't just stand there, come in!"

She tidies the room. Pulls the covers over the unmade bed. Stands facing Raphaël after she has taken the flowers from him. She seems lost, as if roused from sleep. So deep a night, she thinks. She pulls the bathrobe across her chest.

"Raphaël dear, if you only knew . . ."

She would like to tell him that the city is liberated, that she is only waiting for him so she can visit the city from top to bottom, no longer protecting herself, now denying nothing.

He seems embarrassed, says again that Céleste is waiting for him. Now he is walking over to the window. He looks out onto the street.

Flora Fontanges looks out too. Shields her eyes with her hand to protect herself from the excess of light. She sees Céleste who is pacing across from the hotel, her long legs like stilts.

She turns towards Raphaël, gold from the sun, far removed from anything but the movements of Céleste down below on the sidewalk.

She can't help appealing to him, to no purpose, and well aware of it:

"I have to tell you something, Raphaël dear."

He is there but not there, and it's pointless for her to act as if she wants to join him in his perfect complicity with Céleste. He is pulled out of Flora Fontanges's room by a tall girl who strides along the pavement like a heron escaped from its swamps.

She wants to hold him back, fears more than anything a relapse into solitude. She looks drawn. She pulls her robe across her chest. She laughs too loud. Turns away from Raphaël. Laughs more softly. Seeks the right tone. Adjusts her robe and her laugh. Assumes a suitable expression. Changes expression without his seeing it. He looks at her back, still shaking with laughter.

"I'm trying to catch my breath," she manages to say.

And already the voice is different, more sonorous and rounded now, almost youthful.

She comes towards him, strange and mysterious. As if illuminated. She takes the little bouquet from the bed. Flora Fontanges brings her face down, over the flowers, breathes the fresh smell of summer on her burning face. Her lips are dry. Her voice has inflections both tender and mocking.

Flower, spring, rebirth

"Buttercups, daisies, vetch, yarrow, white clover, pink clover."

Her cascading laughter. She approaches Raphaël. She seems to have a priceless secret for him.

"Good my lord,/How does your honor for this many a day?"
Raphaël's smile is frozen.

"So please you, something touching the lord Hamlet."
She lets the flowers fall to the ground.

"I would give you some violets but they withered all."
Her voice cracks again.

"Go, Raphaël dear, quickly now, you mustn't keep Céleste waiting."

She asks to be told as soon as Maud is found.

All at once she sounds as if she is losing her voice.

THE CHAMBERMAIDS ARE PES-
tering her. Knock on the door every ten minutes. Ask
over and over if they can make up the room. Might as
well leave these crumpled sheets, this hastily tidied room.
Tackle the city alone. Since Raphaël has gone away with
Céleste and she is as lonely as on Judgement Day.

As for rue Plessis, all of that takes place in her head. The
dazzle of the day sweeps into the wide-open window on
rue Sainte-Anne, but another street, dark and narrow,
persists in her memory, its blackness and narrowness suddenly brightened by a doorknob of cut glass.

One day, unique in the world, a long slender hand
gloved in black kid grasped that doorknob glittering like
a precious stone, pure marvel for a little girl.

The door was opened at once for the lady from the
Esplanade, who began to climb the steps, very slowly,
lifting her cashmere skirt lest she pick up any bad smells
on the staircase.

The old lady observed the clutter in their lodgings and
recommended they would be well-advised to sell off some
of their useless furniture. After she took the little girl from
the sitting room and was sure that she wasn't listening at

the door, she described the assistance she proposed to
offer her daughter and her fallen son-in-law. Responsibility
for Madame Eventurel's clothing, for her hats and linens,
would be assumed by her mother for the duration of
Monsieur Eventurel's difficulties. For the rest, they need
only carry on as if nothing has changed and hold their
heads high as if they were not living on rue Plessis. The
old lady intends to play the game herself at the proper
time, and organize a grand ball in her house on the
Esplanade in honour of this little girl who has no name,
obtaining for her at one stroke the pretext needed to
establish her in the city. The old lady from the Esplanade
would be glad to lend the Eventurel name to Pierrette
Paul for one season, for the time needed to find a husband.
And the end of the Eventurels' good deed that was begun
one night during a fire would be marked by the sound
of the wedding march.

She is eighteen years old. She has been told that the pearls
around her neck have come down to her grandmother.
She pretends to believe it, and the others around her
keep up the pretence. But no one is fooled. This is a
small provincial town where everyone knows everything
and has since the beginning of time.

The house on the Esplanade is all lit up, from cellar
to attic, even the small dormer windows on the third floor
which look like the glowing tips of minuscule cigarettes
in the night.

A tall lady wearing black silk and shining jet receives,
elegant and haughty. Imposture and ridicule, she thinks
deep down. Laughs. Old she-wolf's teeth in an emaciated
face . . . She is giving a ball in honour of her false grand-
daughter, as if she were real. She tells her: "Good evening,
Marie," naming her for the first time. She kisses her
forehead for the first time. She is thumbing her nose at the
entire city. She is offering a spectacle of pomp and excess.

A long white glove, just faintly yellow, lifeless, like a dead snake found lying across a road. Is it all that remains of a season of parties and balls? Flora Fontanges drinks her second Martini, sipping it. Around her, muted conversations. Cigarette smoke drifts through the hotel bar in great blue scrolls. Green glints. Aquarium atmosphere.

Once there were two long ball gloves, quite alive, with three small mother-of-pearl buttons where the wrist begins, on the palm side. Compelling fragrance. Soft against the skin. Silver sandals. Flowers in her hair.

Never has the Eventurels' adopted daughter seemed closer to the heart and to the dearest wishes of her adoptive parents. Slender and straight in her long white gown, she looks altogether like someone who wants to be part of society.

The debutantes, hair waved and curled, family jewels around necks and wrists, showing décolletés for the first time, clutch handfuls of skirts made of faille, taffeta, silk, tulle and muslin, or let them trail on the floor which has been sprinkled with boric acid to make it slipperier.

The boys, buttoned into freshly pressed tuxedos, very straight parts in short hair slicked with brilliantine, make the debutantes dance till dawn.

The luckiest will marry within the year.

She danced for one whole winter, losing herself in the dance as if she were singing or reciting poems. Her body grew lighter and lighter, given over to the arms of her dancing partners, then transfixed once again as soon as the dance was done, resuming then the pose of a well brought-up young lady. She would have liked to become a dancer and to make the entire world ring out under her heels, like a hard, smooth dance floor edged with trees and vast rivers.

At the end of the third month of parties and balls the worst dancer in town asked her to marry him and she said no. It's easy to say no, like that, to a boy who has trodden on your feet all winter, especially if his expression is sullen and sly, surprised by the no that she uttered, sharp and clear. But what's most difficult is explaining that in order to live one needs an enormous dance floor, where nothing can limit the momentum and shut in the heart, and that the dreamed-of love is not to be found here.

M. and Mme Eventurel are simply amazed. Such a good catch, a lawyer's only son, heir to his father's practice, and such a neat little black mustache, like Charlie Chaplin's.

Too confined in her skin, which is cracking from top to bottom, Marie Eventurel feels like a little lizard, warmed by the sun, who moults and leaves behind his wilted scales. For the first time, she does not play at being the perfect adopted daughter. Her honesty is unsparing. She declares in a steady voice:

"I don't want to marry, not with any boy. I want to work on stage, and I've decided to leave here and choose a name that will be my very own."

She was called ungrateful and shameless. The theatre was an invention of the devil, unworthy of a girl of good society. The break occurred at one stroke, between her and her adoptive parents, as if preparations for it had been made in advance, in the shadows, like a piece of cloth worn by air and sun which tears seemingly of its own volition in our astonished hands. They raised no objections to her emancipation, though she was only eighteen. She left town on the *Empress of Britain*, as a chambermaid. Her experience of poverty became her most precious possession, along with patience, of which she turned out to have a great deal. What awaited her, on the other side of the ocean, was at once more beautiful and fiercer than anything she could imagine. To learn one's craft, to become oneself *full-blown and on all sides exposed to the sun* and to find every day the money necessary for the most rudimentary existence.

She is on her third Martini. There is too much smoke here. The air becomes visible, greenish and heavy, it blends with the smoke. A sort of magma wherein people float like dead fish.

Flora Fontanges experiences the deaths of her adoptive parents like a foreboding, as if these deaths were going to occur at any moment, before her eyes, having not yet caught up with her, fixed in her heart in 1956 when she realized she had no tears or sorrow and felt ungrateful and light, all absorbed in playing *Miss Julie* in the French provinces.

Nothing is alive here now, in this bar. The atmosphere becomes more and more rarefied. The present no longer exists. All these people bent over their drinks are like accidental light in the murky water of a pond. The imperious welling of tears. The news of the deaths of her adoptive parents, occurring a few weeks apart, comes to her across time and space. She sees again the blue paper of the telegram, the small black letters dance before her eyes. The burning sensation of stinging tears. She covers her smarting eyes with her hands. Tells herself it is irreparable. It has happened. Is happening at this very moment. The deaths of her adoptive parents. She weeps. She will probably never know if they secretly loved one another, for just one moment, M. and Mme Eventurel and she. Lacking a sure memory, she has only her tears.

Now she is out on the street in the middle of the night, in the rain, although since she arrived here she has not dared take a step in the city by herself. Côte de la Couronne. Why not settle matters now? She has only delayed them too long. Climb to the top of this steep hill, to the place where . . . It is a decision she made when she was still in the hotel bar, warmed by alcohol and driven outside by the bar's stuffy atmosphere, her loneliness, too, pushing her towards an ever greater solitude.

The rain trickles down her face and onto her neck, a slow summer rain filled with a mixture of scents. The city baked by summer steams in the night, under the rain, wet pavement, exhaust fumes, dust, and soot, while now and again surprising fragrances of earth, grass, and leaves, from who knows where, come to her in great swathes filled with sweetness.

My courage is supreme, she repeats to herself, hands thrust deep in the pockets of her raincoat. I am drunk with courage and alcohol, she thinks. She laughs to herself as she hurries down the hill. A comfortable warmth in her veins while her rain-wet face stays cool, like a rose, she notes with satisfaction. The passage from warmth to coolness on her skin. The voluptuous delight of a summer evening in the rain. She is a stranger now, walking in a strange city.

At first she does not recognize Côte de la Couronne, never having seen it at night or in her present state of mild intoxication. Alternating great dark gaps and neon lights. An unfamiliar avenue lined with banners by turns dark or dazzling. Nothing palpable or solid, *trompe l'oeil* houses that sway at the edge of sidewalks, above all nothing recognizable that might show her she is going down towards the heart of the forbidden city.

The war or some other equally brutal calamity has passed this way. It is filled with abandoned buildings and with barely camouflaged demolitions. She must have turned right without realizing it. Here is boulevard Charest, or is it rue Saint-Joseph? Everywhere, the disorder of a city that cannot show its proper face but smashes it instead, as if it were a pleasure to put out an eye or break a nose. The department stores have been moved to the suburbs. The neighbourhood is disused. The air one breathes smells of ashes and chalk. Entire streets have been shaken like rugs, their buildings broken like toys.

She must retrace her steps. Climb back up Côte de la Couronne. Has vowed she will go to the end of this endless hill. Desires with an unvarying desire to get to the bottom of her memory. Soon the dark mass of an unfamiliar building blocks her way.

She is determined, though, to stay there in front of this strange façade, where no sign of life or death is addressed to her. The whole city is silent and cheerless, like stagnant water. No one can awaken what no longer exists. Pointless to dig under this new building, darker than the surrounding night, where one will find only time past and charred ruins.

It is there that in another time stood the Hospice

Saint-Louis. How calm and smooth everything is here, she
thinks, hands in the pockets of her trench coat, hair
standing up on her head like a kingfisher emerging from
the water. Her faint memory weighs no more than a dead
leaf. The warmth of her present life keeps vigil in her
veins.

Now images are looming up at the speed of the wind,
faster than thought, a wild quickness, while the five senses,
stirred to life, bring sounds, smells, touch, bitter tastes
which unloose memories, precise arrows drawn from the
shadows, without respite.

The present no longer concerns Flora Fontanges.

It is a fortress for women and children, hermetically sealed
in the winter night. The surrounding city can very well
make and unmake itself as it wishes, nothing and no one
comes through the fence around the hospice except on
visiting days and according to terms carefully laid down
in regulations.

December 14, 1927.

Everyone inside is asleep, thirty nuns, three hundred
seventy-one little girls aged from five to twelve.

No fire extinguisher, no fire escape, no night watchman,
no fire drill. "The Lord is my shepherd," sing the girls in
chorus, before they go to sleep, while Sister Saint-Amable
declares that not one hair can fall from their heads without
divine permission.

Half-past ten. Already the first sign of fire flares in a
dormer window on the top floor.

A man is coming home from the arena after a hockey
game. The snow creaks under his feet. White mist emerges
from his mouth with every breath. He looks up. Sees the
flames at the window. Sounds the alarm.

A night light sheds its muted glow along a dormitory

where fifty little girls sleep in iron beds lined against the walls on either side. They sleep, and already their dreams are filled with visions of fire and terror. From there to crossing the line into wakefulness and finding death beside one's bed, it is just one step. The burning bush, the unbearable face of God hidden in the heart of the flames, Ishmael's thirst in the desert, the Egyptians' first-born who are put to death, the sacrifice of Isaac, the fiery tongues of Pentecost, and the glowing fires of the inferno that await little girls who don't behave themselves, ah! above all the inferno . . .

"Please God don't let me die tonight in a state of mortal sin!"

The fire rumbles from floor to floor like a furious wind. The smoke is more and more dense. Bells are rung in the corridors. People shout: "Fire! Fire!" from dormitory to dormitory.

Children, children, thinks Sister Saint-Amable, evoking Jesus Christ lamenting Jerusalem, and she wishes she could gather them all around her skirts like chicks and take them from here, all these children who are entrusted to her care.

Wailing, tears. Someone clutches her dressing gown. They want to believe it is she who is the absolute mistress of our life and of our death. To obey her, once again.

Their old terrors are behind the door that opens onto the hallway, their tongues of fire pass beneath the door. A distraught woman in a dressing gown who claims to be our Sister Saint-Amable wants to take us with her, make us walk through the flames, then throw us, half-naked, into the snow and the night, when we do not know what night is, having seen it only surreptitiously, through a window, having never been inside it, having heard about the shadows where there is wailing and gnashing of teeth, and the snow that lies motionless under our windows, cold below, blazing above, the snow that we already know and that is unforgiving, we must obey and leave this place, the fire runs across the floor as if someone has broken a thermometer, the smoke stings our eyes and throat. Mother, how frightening you are, and trembling, without your solemn garments! We must go with you, at once, before, Mother, Mother . . .

Now the electricity blows and the children, gathered together with great difficulty, scream, scatter, run every which way, amid the smoke and the dark. Some seek shelter in their beds, huddling under their blankets.

It was impossible to get them out, sobs Sister Saint-Amable who has joined the other nuns on the snow, in a shivering cluster whence come instructions, incoherent and vain, addressed to the firemen.

Sister Marie-des-Neiges has saved six little girls and the holy species of the Eucharist.

Who now would dare to cross the blazing coals except Rosa Gaudrault, who has offered the gift of her life?

Thirty-six little girls perished in the fire, as did Rosa Gaudrault who was their maid and their first teacher.

While it is true that all the nuns were saved, the real miracle is that, intact in the smoking debris, was found the head of the statue of Saint Louis of Gonzaga.

R<small>INGS OF FLAME TO PASS</small>
through, as in the circus. Has she not been a circus
performer all her life? And now it is beginning again.
Rehearsals for *Happy Days* get under way tomorrow. Already, her name is Winnie. Trial by fire once again.
Crossing the line. The first time, she was in the arms
of a helmeted man when she passed through a window
filled with sparks, and her old name, Pierrette Paul,
stayed behind her, to be consumed like ash in the flames
of the Hospice Saint-Louis. It crackles and rumbles at
her back, and it is the breathing of death that sniffs
and licks her. A man carries her outside, onto the snow,
like a bundle, climbs back onto his tall ladder to bring
out another screaming little girl. Someone in the night
declares that henceforth her name is Marie Eventurel.
She will subsequently prove that there will be no end
to jumping into the midst of the flames. Circus life is
filled with risks and with incomparable jubilation when
she passes through the shattered nucleus of her heart,
in blazing flakes of fire. I am Phaedra, Célimène, Ophelia,
Desdemona. I land on my feet after each performance.
Bow very low. Then go about my business like everybody
else.

The director of the Emérillon told her:

"You must fill the whole stage, be full as an egg, on the verge of shattering, as if your ribs were going to break and split apart. Your partner's presence depends on you, on the attention you pay to his almost invisible existence. You create him in a sense, his day-to-day existence depends on yours, which must be lying in wait for his slightest movement."

"Oh this is going to be another happy day!"

"Hail, holy light!"

"This will have been another happy day!"

One needs the memory of an elephant to remember it all. Sentence fragments come and go, never altogether the same, reappear half swallowed. Above all, do not lose sight of the thread of despair which links the short simple sentences into a paltry necklace.

The props! Good Lord, the props! She must learn to use the props along with the words. The play of props overlaps the play of words, as when the fingers of the right hand are interlaced with the left.

Parasol, spectacles, capacious black bag, toothbrush, toothpaste, handkerchief, flask, lipstick, mirror, bottle of medicine, lipstick, mirror, brimless hat, magnifying-glass, postcard.

She has laid all the objects in a careful row on her bedspread. She examines them now with a sort of fervent lust, wanting to appropriate them for herself at once.

image of
pirette & grandmother

MAUD HAS COME BACK. COLLAPSED
at her mother's feet in the little hotel room. She is crying.
Asks to be forgiven. Her flowered cotton skirt spread out
on the floor. She hugs Flora Fontanges's legs in both arms.
Lays her head on Flora Fontanges's lap. Wishes she could
melt away between her mother's knees. Disappear. Recover
the perfect union, the innocence of the time before she
drew her first breath in the human world.

I've come back because of you, just for you . . .

Flora Fontanges says: "my little girl." Says again "my
little girl," her voice almost absent, a mere breath, barely
audible, murmurs over and over into Maud's hair: "my
little girl, my little girl."

"It's finished with Raphaël. I never want to see him
again."

Maud has straightened up. Her eyelids are red, and the
tip of her nose. A long black braid flaps against her back.

She explains that the three of them ran into one another
at Tadoussac. She saw right away there was something
between Céleste and Raphaël, and that she cannot bear.

"Take me with you, far far away. I don't want to stay
here."

She looks at the props on the bed, says they're pathetic,

143

that Winnie is no role for Flora Fontanges.

"I don't want you to play a broken-down old woman. I want to go away with you, far from here. Start life over with you. An ordinary, comfortable life for the two of us, in your garret in Touraine if you want. We'll have a garden and a dog and cat, turtledoves and a coffee grinder . . . we'll travel too, I suppose, maybe Greece . . ."

Flora Fontanges shuts her eyes. Wishes she could lose herself in Maud's kind words. Forget the little parasol on the bed, and the brimless hat with faded flowers that awaits her. Not to think. Pack her bags. To leave, now. Take her daughter. Start life over with Maud as if she were not the cruellest of children. Pretend to believe in the possibility of regaining a lost paradise. The first days of Maud's life rediscovered. To relive them again. Only once. For a moment. Just for a moment. Before going back to the real world with all its constraints and commitments. Flora Fontanges cannot forget the contract she has signed with the Emérillon, while the role of Winnie is already stirring in her, laying claim to the continuation of a life barely begun. Enough to make Maud infinitely jealous, she thinks, as if Flora Fontanges were carrying another child in her womb.

She knows she is awkward and risks spoiling everything by asking questions that are too direct. A mere nothing could get Maud's back up and make her run away again. She'll never know why Maud left Raphaël the first time. She won't ask.

Maud has gathered everything on the bed into her mother's paisley shawl and pulled together the corners. She says that everything's set for their departure, and that life requires sacrifices and shedding excess baggage. She makes as if to throw the bundle out the window. She is laughing very hard.

Flora Fontanges has phoned to order tea and cakes.

They drink tea together: two ladies on a social call

observing one another surreptitiously and weighing their words between sips. Flora Fontanges explains that she cannot leave before September. Maud agrees to wait until Flora Fontanges is ready to go. Very peaceably, they plan their return to Touraine.

After a lengthy silence, Maud suddenly gets up and starts to sing the praises of mathematics. Flora Fontanges understands her to say that nothing in the world is purer than mathematics. Maud remains standing, very straight, braced in a sort of fierce determination.

"I wasted too much time with Raphaël. Now I must devote myself to my education."

Her impenetrable gaze, its blue steadiness rimmed in black. Like a cold flame. Her porcelain pallor, despite the summer sun.

Flora Fontanges has just enough time to take her daughter away. They should leave at once. Quickly, before Maud changes her mind. And here she is preparing the bed next to hers, in the hotel room on rue Sainte-Anne. Delivers her daughter to sleep. Postpones any decision until tomorrow. Contents herself with dreaming at her sleeping daughter's bedside, watching over her in the dark, attentive to the regular sound of her breathing. Maud has just come back to her, and now she recites to herself, like a prayer, the last sentence of *Le Grand Meaulnes*:

"And already I was imagining him some night, wrapping his daughter in a cloak and setting off with her towards new adventures."

Maud is a cold flame while Flora is the one consumed by flames.

religious iconology
Eric as false christ

Eric HAS DECIDED TO CELEBRATE
Maud's return. Here they are all together around the
kitchen table, concerned that the meal they have carefully
prepared should go well. Couscous with chicken and lamb:
a change from their usual millet and tofu. Flora Fontanges
has brought wine, Céleste a big bowl of wild raspberries
from her trip to Charlevoix.

Céleste at one end of the table, Raphaël at the other.
He seems not to know her and carefully avoids looking
at her. Maud is beside a pimply boy who goes out of his
way to graze her shoulder or hand, apologizing every time,
his manner both embarrassed and delighted.

She looks at them and listens to them, these boys and
girls, and at her own daughter who is one of them. It's
almost as if they were talking and gesticulating behind a
glass. She is on the other side of the glass with her
unfamiliar life, like old currency no longer legal tender,
in some unknown country. Shadows behind a glass, she
thinks, and the darkest of those shadows is unquestionably
Maud, her daughter, who is eluding her again, all complete
within her mystery, lost in a secret society with its singular
customs and rituals.

As for Eric, the only son of wealthy parents, Flora

146

Fontanges's surprise has no limits. It strikes her that he is playing at poverty, like Christ leaving his father's Paradise to assume the human condition. Perhaps Eric, too, has some original sin to be forgiven by the city's poor who have been gravely offended from the beginning of time?

Eric says that mercury has been found in the body of a salmon caught in the Saguenay, that if this goes on the entire earth will be nothing but pollution and waste.

Céleste says we won't save the earth from destruction by living as if it were the year one thousand, and that the atomic bomb is available to anyone who knows how to use it.

Eric declares that a certain way of life, which may seem archaic, is still our only recourse in the face of the progressive dehumanization of a world given over to machines. Eric dreams of divesting himself of artifice and of being restored to man's original poverty, to the free exercise of all his rekindled senses. It is a dream he would share with all those with him now who listen in silence as if his remarks, although familiar, were being clearly uttered tonight for the first and only time, though frequently summarized and contemplated in the obscurity of each person's heart, down the length of the days . . .

Eric's voice is slow and deep, with muffled vibrations. It is compelling and it carries to the heart.

Eric lowers his head, his long smooth hair falls on either side of his face. He appears to be blessing the meal and the guests, and the guests too feel that they are blessed and confirmed in grace by Eric.

Silence, for a moment, remains upon them like peace.

The first to rise is Céleste. She asks, in a powerful voice: "Who wants a glass of milk?"

They have abandoned their half-full glasses of wine and dived into tall glasses of cold milk as if quenching their thirst on the first morning of the world.

Maud and Raphaël have slipped away behind the glass

bead curtain that separates the kitchen from the room beside it. The curtain is raised, then falls amid a clinking rain of beads. Through the thin screen of multicoloured balls Maud and Raphaël can be heard talking sotto voce.

In one leap Céleste is at the front door, slamming it violently before she disappears into the night.

E<small>VERY NIGHT WHEN SHE RETURNS</small> to the hotel after rehearsal, Maud is there waiting. Before the door is even fully open, Flora Fontanges calls out:

"Maud, are you there?"

Maud kisses her on the cheeks, forehead, nose, neck. Declares that she hasn't moved all day. Mathematics alone has kept her company. Sometimes she adds that Raphaël called and that she hung up immediately. She says Raphaël with a sort of strange diligence, as if the name cannot totally blend into the sentence, but remains separate, deserving another fate. She goes on quickly:

"Don't worry, Mother dear. Nothing bad can happen to us now. I'm your prisoner. While I wait for Touraine. I'm fastened to this room, my two feet sunk in your carpet. The whole city, including Raphaël, could collapse under my windows and I wouldn't budge."

That great stillness spreads through the room. Flora Fontanges and her daughter rest, lying one beside the other, pretending not to feel the obscure menace that prowls in the dark air. Maud sometimes weeps in the middle of the night, causing her mother to wake with a start. She says her tears aren't real, but dream tears, tells her to pay no attention to them. In the morning, it all seems forgotten, and Maud wolfs down her breakfast as if it were the only thing in the world that was genuine.

How many days shut away in a hotel room, how many nights of dream weeping did it take to bring Maud to this intense agitation that makes her spring to her feet at her mother's arrival? Her freshly washed hair is pasted against her shoulders and back, she smells of soft water and shampoo. Her pale face seems smaller, as if cramped, like a closed fist. Her too wide-open eyes shine as if she has a fever.

Despite her fatigue, Flora Fontanges wants to resume the everyday acts that, for some time now, have united her to her daughter, night after night, in the little hotel room on rue Sainte-Anne. Why not trust to the force of habit, weave it patiently around Maud like a slender spider's web, to hold her for a little while yet?

She need only act as if nothing has happened, neither Maud's strange fever nor her abrupt movements nor her way of suddenly talking too loud and gesticulating for no reason.

Flora Fontanges arranges her daughter's hair for the night, braiding it like a little girl's. Maud grows impatient. Says she's going to have her hair cut tomorrow and Raphaël won't recognize her. She becomes voluble and moves incessantly in the cluttered room. She talks about the soft light of Touraine and the pleasant, ordinary life they'll live there, on the banks of the Loire. Without transition she declares that no one in the world walks like Raphaël and that no one in the world has teeth as white as Raphaël's. She says that, and she looks out the window. She appears to want to challenge someone invisible who might be hidden in the city. She is out of breath and is speaking louder and louder. Leaves the window. Approaches her mother, who is sitting on the

Maud searches for stability

bed. Declares that she can't stand being shut up and wants
to go out.

Maud undoes her wet braids. Dons a red mini-skirt and
white boots. Her long bare legs. The small bag slung over
her shoulder.

"Come on, Mama, hurry, we're going out! Hurry up,
you're coming with me!"

Then begins a tour of the city such as Flora Fontanges
has never experienced.

Avenues filled with people in the heat of the night. The
glorious summer night riddled with stars. The maze of
little streets. Blinking signs. Discothèques come into view
here and there along the streets, from the largest to the
smallest, some of them tiny and half-hidden under an
outside staircase, dug into the earth like mouse holes.
Maud goes from one to the next, unable to decide. Makes
comparisons as she goes. Opens doors just a crack. Hazards
a glance. Gusts of sound, muffled throbbing, clouds of
smoke rise up to her face, while her cheeks, her nose,
her forehead reflect the colours of all the lights.

This is a girl who has sworn she'll explode, all alone,
in the music and the noise, a free and independent creature.
She has laid this odd bet, to take a tired old woman along
with her, as a witness. She pulls her by the hand. At every
club, Maud shrinks back, shakes her head, then takes off
again with Flora Fontanges on her heels.

Sometimes Maud looks behind her, over her shoulder.
She claims someone's been following her since the hotel.

It's not that the deep and noisy retreat where Maud is
engulfed with Flora Fontanges seems reassuring, but they
must go inside somewhere to escape the boy who is hidden
in the darkness and has been shadowing the two women
since the hotel, maintaining just enough distance so they
never see his face. Only his feline gait gives him away.

FLORA FONTANGES IS HURLED INTO
the sound and the fury of life. It vibrates all through her
body. She is like a drum that reverberates as it is struck.
A little more and her ribs will shatter, her heart spring
loose and fall to her feet, under the violence of the
repeated shocks. Flora Fontanges presses her hands to
her ears. Feels barbarous spasms in her chest. She looks
on, as in a dream, under the green rays of light, as the
boys and girls break loose, appear and disappear in the
convulsive movements of the shimmering light. Their
solitude particularly surprises her, she who has been
accustomed to couples dancing in each other's arms.
What are they doing on the dance floor, all of them
separate, showing off as they undulate and sway their
hips?

Maud stands utterly still, as if plunged in meditation.
Her whole body picks up energy and rhythm. The beat
is swallowed up by all the pores of her skin, like a storm,
it makes her bones ring and her blood throb.

Presently she steps onto the minuscule dance floor,
grazing the other dancers without looking at them, avoid-
ing them, threading her way through them, clearing a
path, following her own thoughts, alone in the world,

in a magma of streaming bodies, of flashes of light and heat, of raw desire on display.

Now he appears in the doorway, lets his tall stature and his handsome face be seen, makes his way unguarded. His clear precise features. His archangel's name which she cannot stop herself from uttering now as he moves towards her from the back of the room. Glides through the dancers until he is facing her. A moment of utter stillness, a wall of ice between them. She is the first to start to move again in rhythm, and he follows each of her moves, silently begging for her forgiveness and her dancer's complicity. A very small space for their steps which already fit together without their knowing, moved by the same obsessive rhythm. A very small space between their foreheads, their mouths, their chests, bellies, hands, which move in rhythm, never joining, a furious attention to the rock music which possesses them equally, their separation and estrangement utterly gone and restored now in the unity of the dance as they face one another, never touching even with a fingertip, pierced by the same arrows, existing powerfully, in a single breath of life, while desire gradually rises and overcomes them.

They drink cool beer, mop their brows, calm down slowly, as if nothing has occurred between them, in this room, nothing at least that they want to talk about, while their hearts seek each other in silence.

Maud and Raphaël accompany Flora Fontanges through the streets of the city to her hotel. They take her arm, they touch her shoulder, with infinite acts of kindness and care, as if she were made of glass and they fear seeing her shatter in their hands at any moment. They disappear very quickly into the night.

When Maud came back to the hotel the next morning,

Flora Fontanges was still in bed, half dreaming, foundering in unshed tears, like dry sand, burning her eyes with them.

She props herself on her pillow and asks for breakfast. Maud pours coffee and butters toast. Says Raphaël and she are reconciled and are ready to start life together again.

The coffee in the steaming cups smells good. Outside, the city is peacefully beginning another summer day of heat and light.

Flora Fontanges has started to leaf through the worn and dog-eared pages of *Happy Days.*

Hail, holy light!

Bitterness and scorn, she thinks. The deepest solitude comes towards her, barely emerging from the magnificent day.

This is going to be a happy day!

And it is Winnie who speaks through the mouth of Flora Fontanges. This woman already knows the four seasons of life when an extra season is given to her, transfiguring everyday joys and sorrows to make of them a violent form of speech that bursts on the stage, in full light.

ON OPENING NIGHT THE THEATRE is filled with spectators, somewhat uncomfortable and vaguely anxious. Embarrassed smiles cannot tilt into laughter. Irritating little coughs. Above it all, the tireless voice of Flora Fontanges tells a story these people would prefer not to hear. Probably they have heard before about the treacherous body and soul, but always accompanied by the proper ritual, sentimental and dramatic, and the long sob of violins to lull their hearts. Tonight, what gloomy ceremony is this, with these meagre props, these pitiable creatures? The spell of Flora Fontanges's voice, though it is broken, her profound conviction act upon them, in their final entrenchment, in this place where they can see themselves in a mirror, for a flash, unrecognizable, suddenly bared, ridiculous, and condemned. *the stage is a mirror.*

They brought down the house, because of the performance they say, then were angry with her for her poisoned gift.

Two of the critics maintained that this was not a play for a summer theatre, and that even if Madame Fontanges was splendid, she could not make them believe in the futility of all things, when the bright July sun was blazing over the world.

The curtain is barely down and they are there backstage, to embrace her. Raphaël's prickly cheek, Maud's as smooth as a baby's. She takes off her makeup and she trembles. The traces of *Happy Days* are inscribed on her face, in lines more enduring than the greasepaint. Maud begs her to remove it all, quickly, and to wash her face with soap and water. She says:

"I don't like you to be old!"

Raphaël repeats:

"You're fantastic . . ."

He appears to be embarrassed by his emotion and seems somewhat aloof from her now. It's all over between them, the sweet familiarity that held them together for long days. She is alone again. She made her tour of the forbidden city, including the Côte de la Couronne and Saint-Roch, without her appointed guide. If you only knew, Raphaël dear, she wants to tell him. But it is to her daughter that she turns now, a little girl so busy listening to her own heart, stolen by Raphaël.

She explains to Maud all the horror that filled her just now, when she picked up the parasol and it wouldn't open.

For a month, she plays Winnie every night except Tuesday, suffering a thousand deaths and a thousand sorrows. She is possessed. She quivers with Winnie's passion and cannot sleep at night, for the plague of small bitter waves that strip her and wear her down, one by one.

At the end of the month, her contract finished, the two of them came to take her to the same country station at which she had arrived. They said goodbye, looking vaguely embarrassed.

She left the city. *The separation has already occurred and the exile into which she enters follows her.* While in her bag, a letter from Paris offering her the part of Mme Frola in *Right You Are* makes her want to laugh and cry at once, like a musical instrument that you graze with your hand, and it vibrates in secret, amid the silence of the earth.